I0666542

Write Where We Are

WriteOn Joliet Third Anthology 2019

By WriteOn Joliet

Cover art by Mauverneen (Maureen) Blevins

Write Where We Are, Copyright © 2019 by WriteOn Joliet
All rights reserved.

PRINTED IN THE UNITED STATES OF AMERICA

No part of this book may be reproduced or transmitted by any means, mechanical or
electronic, including photocopying, recording, or by any information storage and retrieval
system, without the written consent of the author. For more information, contact
writeonJolietgroup@gmail.com

Cover art by Mauverneen (Maureen) Blevins

ISBN 978-1-949777-11-6

www.writeonjoliet.com

WriteOn Joliet anthology 2019 contributors: Denise M. Baran-Unland, Mauverneen Blevins, Holly Coop, Diana Estell, Annette Gonzales, Alfredo Gutierrez, Robert Hafey, Dale Hansen, Jessica Harris, Ryan Harris, Tom Hernandez, Todd Hogan, S. Houk, R. Michael Markley, Kenneth Lee McGee, Sue Mydliak, James Pressler, Colleen H Robbins, Allison Rios, Jennifer Russ, Vanessa J.C. Stephens, Duanne Walton

All your previous days
Existed
To prepare you
For this
Particular
Day.

-S. Houk

ABOUT WRITEON JOLIET

WriteOn started as WriteOn Minooka, co-founded by Denise M. Baran-Unland and Kristina Skaggs. Our members come from all over the southern suburbs.

Some have self-published or have been traditionally published. Others are still exploring their writing options and interests. Regardless of our place in the writing world, WriteOn welcomes everyone looking to write, read and grow.

WriteOn Joliet is a welcoming, diverse group of writers of varied skills, interests and experience. The group includes professional journalists, fiction novelists, bloggers, screenwriters, musicians and poets.

We promise a safe, comfortable and supportive atmosphere to share your work, and constructive feedback so that everyone can benefit from our shared knowledge.

WriteOn is a dues-paying organization. The first visit is free.

For more information, visit www.writeonJoliet.com.

TABLE OF CONTENTS

AFTER LOSING YOU

By Holly Coop

Wearing black cause I'm feeling blue
Lost and lonely after losing you
Time will tell if I'll have strength enough
To get me through the days ahead
For they will be long and rough

Missing, crying, regretting, dying
Are just a few of the adjectives I will use
To describe the way I am feeling after losing you

Life doesn't always prepare us
For when IT chooses to leave
But God promises we can bear it
When we choose to lean on Him and believe

The days are long
The night belongs
To my pillow, it wears my tears
Their deluge held back all day
While I must keep myself in gear

Now the moon allows me to weep
So in my pillow, I bury the grief
While crying myself to sleep

The sun will beckon a tomorrow
To usher in yet another day
That I might refresh in its newness
I know, somewhere in the heavens
For this and for me you pray

After losing you
I'll go on because you'd want me to
On the outside, I will carry on

My grief only visible to *me*
On the inside, I'll be wearing black
Because of the way I feel

After losing you

AUTUMN'S KISS

By Sue Mydliak

There once was a young girl who lived all alone. Claire was her name. All she ever wanted was someone to talk to and to show that they cared.

Day in and day out, she'd walk in the fields just behind the orphanage. It was there and only there that she could be her real and true self, but it still wasn't enough.

It wasn't until a week later that something peculiar happened. She couldn't understand if what she saw was real or a dream, but it excited her.

She was in the kitchen of the orphanage washing the breakfast dishes. You see, everyone had a job to do while they lived there, and dishwashing became hers. As daunting as it seemed, this was her light at the end of a very long tunnel.

"You there! Quit your daydreaming and finish up with those dishes, or you'll have to deal with Mrs. Chesterfield," came the booming voice of Miss Humphreys.

All Claire wanted to do was to tell her just exactly how she felt. She always wanted to speak up and say how cruel and unjust she acted toward her and the others, but — only in her head could she say such things. Even if you were to look at Miss Humphreys in the slightest way, even without knowing, just to look, she would think you were up to no good and that would be a bad mistake indeed.

That alone made Claire think otherwise and to keep her mouth shut. Claire really didn't think that if anyone were to be cruel to her as she was to all the other children, that she would kill them. Secretly. Mysteriously. Unbeknownst to anyone but her. Claire being the sensible girl that she was, knew that they were just stories made up to frighten them . . . but deep down, in the back of her mind, she thought otherwise.

So, being the good child that she was, she did not say a word but continued washing. She pretended as though she was hard at work and kept her head in a downward position so that Miss Humphreys would think she was actually doing her job, even though she'd be daydreaming of places that were beautiful and gloriously wonderful.

When she heard Miss Humphrey's footsteps leave the kitchen and that they got quieter and quieter, did she look out the window once more . . . and there he stood, looking at her. His height only slightly taller than she, black hair, a slim body, and eyes that pierced her very soul. Normally, Claire would blush and look away, but not this time. She couldn't.

Part of her told her to stay and finish her work, while the other told her to go out and see what he wanted. Oh, how she wanted to go out there. She wanted to hear what his voice sounded like. Would it be quiet, soft as a whisper, or would it be gruff . . . no, gruffness didn't suit him at all.

She looked behind her. Went to the kitchen door and peeked down the hallway. No one. Now was her chance to meet him. She shook from the excitement, knowing that she was about to do something so preposterous, so daring, and yet, her heart urged her on.

Without thinking or hesitation, Claire went over to the back door, opened it slowly, and crept out. Making sure that it didn't bang shut. There she stood and there he stood. From that moment on, she would never look back, for she knew with him, it would be fate. They were to meet; she knew it and so did her heart.

The only thing she could hear, as she went forward were her footsteps as she ran across the hardened ground. Within minutes they came face to face. Neither of them said a word, they didn't need to, yet, in this silence so much was said.

She didn't know when it happened, but he had taken her hand, gentle like and held it. It was warm, soft, and she felt complete. Was this love? For if not, she would make it so. She wanted to say so much, but the words never came forth. Almost as if something prevented her from doing so.

They stood, staring, drinking each other in. Time stopped and all around them, everything ceased to exist. For all they saw, were themselves. Nothing else mattered, not now or any other time. For it was at that precise moment, that she would be his forever.

With her hand in his, he bent forward, as in a bow, and kissed hers. Such a bold move, especially when they were never properly introduced. Did she care? No, in fact, Claire rather liked it. His lips, like a rose petal, were soft.

Could this be really happening? She thought. It felt as though she were in a dream. A beautiful dream, one that she hoped would never end.

He began to lead her toward a path that led into the woods. Claire hesitated. His face confused and saddened, urged her on. How could she not? He would not harm her, and she felt that way as well. After a few brief minutes, she went with him.

She didn't care where they were going, she just wanted to be with him.

Again, they spoke not a word, as the canopy above them held songbirds who flew and nested within. It wasn't until she heard water running that she became excited. What if there was a waterfall? A great, thunderous waterfall. With luscious flowering plants and trees. She then took it upon herself to lead the way.

The sound of water falling, crashing against rocks became apparent. She was right! Through a small clearing ahead, a giant waterfall greeted them and along the rocks and boulders, exotic flowers bloomed in bright colors of red, yellow and blue. She closed her eyes and breathed in deep. Heaven, so much so, that she wanted to swim in its cool waters.

He pointed toward the water as if to say, go ahead, go in. Claire wondered if she should be so bold. Would he follow her as well? It did not matter. This thrilled her, for she never did anything like this before.

Inching, closer and closer, until she finally placed her foot in first, shoe and all. She giggled and placed the other foot in as well. Such delights that she squealed out loud. Finding the courage to go in farther, she crept. The nippiness caught her breath and she shivered but kept going until she stood waist deep.

This had to be the most thrilling thing ever. There she stood, in waist deep water, with the most charming boy she'd ever seen and didn't care how she looked. In fact, she didn't care so much so, that she began to splash about, for she felt so gay!

"Claire . . . Claire . . . CLAIRE!"

Startled Claire shook and found herself in the kitchen. Water running everywhere and she, herself, soaked to the skin.

"What in all that is holy are you doing? Look at this mess! Shut the water off immediately and clean this up quickly! As for dinner, you shall have none."

Quite surprised herself, she turned the water off. What had happened? Did she dream this, or did it really happen? It baffled her, but as she went to reach for a towel, she found a beautiful, red exotic flower . . . like the one in the woods . . . next to the waterfall.

BEAUTIFUL SIGNATURE

By Colleen H. Robbins

Trevor picked up the pen. The gnarled muscles of his right arm cramped, and the pen dropped from suddenly nerveless fingers. He glanced up at the clock. Only ten minutes before the signing.

#

His handwriting had once been beautiful, flowing from his right hand so easily. "Blessed by God," his mother told everyone. Perhaps that was the problem.

His father glowered at him. "Put down the book and get in the truck. Mrs. Grady's garden needs weeding." Mrs. Grady. One of the Big House people who employed his father to keep their properties looking nice. The same people who looked at him--and his father--as though they were bugs.

At sixteen, Trevor started dropping tools. His hand cramped and arm shook so violently that he could no longer safely weed. A month later, when his hand curled into a weak, unusable mass, Trevor's father took him to the clinic.

The doctors shook their heads. "Carpal Tunnel," they finally said, then gave him pain killers and a special glove to wear. "Don't use the arm for a few weeks."

"It's a curse, put on your arm by a witch." Mama spent two hours a day at church, praying for him. She came home smelling like incense and candles in the evening.

"It's all in your head," his father said, smelling like new grass. "You are ashamed to be the son of a gardener."

#

The arm continued to get worse. The doctors at the clinic tried everything: muscle relaxers, physical therapy, and finally surgery. Nothing helped.

Trevor slowly trained himself to write left-handed. It looked nothing like his right hand's former beauty. Instead, it crawled out of his left hand like an angry centipede stomping across the page. The computers at school, and later in the library, were a godsend. He found a talent for writing stories, mostly horror stories involving insect bites and evil spirits, his parents' latest theories.

He sold a few pieces, and a few more over the years, and the extra income helped to stretch the disability check he got for his arm. And now he had written a book, and in mere seconds he was to sign it. He meant to try and sign it with his right hand, hoping to send the book off with the good luck that his mother's God gave to the right-handed. A beautiful signature would make the book perfect.

#

He carefully propped a pen in his right hand, securing it with a plastic bandage strip, and then another just to be sure. His long sleeves covered the padding he attached to cushion his arm so that he would not bruise the skin if it started to shake. More pens filled his left pocket in case of disaster. He opened a book and smelled the fresh ink on the pages. He closed it reverently and gripped his pen.

When the bookstore doors opened with a jingle, the line at his table grew longer by the second. He had hoped for one, maybe five people to come buy his book. This stampede terrified him. But he managed to control his hand and arm long enough to sign the first, the fifth, and even the twentieth copy. The door jingled and the clock ticked away on the wall as his arm started to twinge. He fumbled the pen once, but the bandage strips kept it tightly in his hand and he recovered.

A salesclerk ambled over, his hair bouncing in the latest style. "We're running out of copies," he whispered. "You'll have to come back next week and sign the rest. We're already giving out coupons with the date."

Another signing? He couldn't do this for much longer, and maybe not ever again. His hand grew numb, but still managed to produce that beautiful signature. But for how long? How far could he push before he damaged the hand too badly? Only five minutes to go.

The door jingled again, and he glanced up to see his father enter the store and stand at the end of the line. His father glowered deeper than ever. Trevor shuddered, and that was all it took. His right arm cramped painfully, curling into itself. The pen flew out of his hand, trailing bandage strips soaked with sweat.

The beautiful signature lay on the page accusing him, half-finished, never to be finished. He cradled his right arm with his left, willing the pain away as he wept.

BOOTS

By Tom Hernandez

This is about boots
Literal and metaphoric
Modern and historic
Like the ones you wear on your evenings out
Walking happily arm in arm to a nice dinner
Together with the one you love
Your boots, comfortable from years of wear
So soft, so warm, so rich, so
Supple and shining with the polish of countless dreams fulfilled
But they pale in comparison to hers
Brown fringe flirting with every dancing step
Bedazzled with diamonds – only the best will do! -- sparkling
In the streetlamp's glow
Miniature moons splitting the chilly night
Lighting the path one step at a time
Toward my shadowy suffering
I pull newspapers around me
praying the ink is as warm now as the words once were
The merciless night mist dampening
My cardboard couch – the only thing between me
And concrete pneumonia
I watch your boots walk by, only raising my eyes
To silently meet your sneer
The blinding glare of your shimmering hypocrisy
Swallowed by the black hole of my reality
Of course, you are right
I should "Pull myself up by my bootstraps"
As (you insist) you did alone, no help from
Anyone! Anywhere! Anytime!
I swear by everything red, white and blue
If I could, I would --
After all, as the song says,
some boots are made for walking
Then I'd spend my evenings just like you

Stomping on and over and around
Everyone who is not Me
Yes sir, Mister Man, I absolutely would --
If only I could afford a pair of boots

COATLICUE

By Annette Gonzales

my ancestral mother
is not a lily white virgin
with downcast eyes
and gentle, praying hands
this creation goddess
casts her eyes downward
for no one
Her noble raiment
a scaly skirt of snakes
a string of bloody hearts
adorn her thick neck
This warrior queen
400 offspring strong
goddess of the ancients
creatrix of sun, moon, and stars
stands alone in her omnipotence
All have knelt before her.
and, now in monolithic state,
her self-contained glory
still commands

"Feel my raiment of snakes,
inhale the stench of these bloody hearts
and
kneel
at
the feet of your true mother!"

CONUNDRUM

By Denise M. Baran-Unland

*Note: This excerpt from the novel "Before the Blood"
examines the conflict between loyalty to one's parents and loyalty
to one's spouse.*

*The late nineteenth century protagonist Bryony Simons,
sheltered until her marriage, is already conflicted regarding her
diet (most of the village is vegetarian; she must eat meat to
preserve her health) and travel (her father never permitted her to
leave the fishing village; she's now visited Chicago and New York
with her husband).*

*"Compromise" is Bryony's survival strategy, until a crisis
occurs, and she struggles make a clear choice.*

Before the Blood, Bryony Simons, Chapter 9: Shattered Glass

*Until the daybreak, and the shadows flee away, turn, my beloved,
and be thou like a roe or a young hart upon the mountains of
Bether. (Song of Solomon, 2:17).*

Dr. Gothart yanked her fingers out of her ears. They
sprang back like a mechanical toy, but he was ready.

"Grab her!"

"Let go! Let go!"

Bryga trapped her arm. Howard pinned her to the bed and
braced her with one knee. Bryony could only work her mouth, so
she used it to scream.

Loud and long and piercing.

Which only intensified the shouting from the first floor.

She smelled the carbolic acid. She felt the stabbing of her
poor little worm. But that's not why she yelled. She knew why
Dr. Gothart wanted her blood.

Apparently, the blood wanted him, too. It eagerly ran out
of her like a thin stream of red water into the vial.

Dr. Gothart untied the cloth. "Release her."

They did, and Bryony wrenched away, fingers clawed, heaving, and glaring at her captors.

"Anything else, Doctor?" Howard asked.

"Yes. Please tell the gentlemen downstairs to voice their opinions a little more softly."

"Straight away."

Howard sped out the door, the fastest Bryony had ever seen the slight man with graying hair move. As John's valet, Howard held himself to high standards. Each bow and nod of the head had grace and purpose.

Once in New York, Bryony had watched Howard shave John. He wielded the blade as Henry a paintbrush, with elegance and fine strokes.

But Bryga looked almost gleeful as she slunk out the door. Her eyes met Bryony's before she crossed the threshold, and she smiled. Some might call it an encouraging smile, but Bryony knew better.

Her father and John still lashed insults and accusations with the ferocity of rival lion tamers. She couldn't discern each word, but the snippets she did catch, "foolhardy," derelict," and "pervert" hinted at the rest.

She rolled onto her side, cradling her head between her hands and drawing her knees up to her belly, which churned like an angry lake.

Dr. Gothart pulled out his pipe and lit it. He puffed and puffed, watching Bryony with an unnerving steadiness.

She closed her eyes and shrank against the bass drum hammering inside her skull, each beat louder than the last.

For years, she breathed in easy, gentle waves. No rocks weighed her head down. Her fingernails grew strong and pink. Her tongue didn't burn. Fish stopped fluttering in her breast.

Until this week.

He removed the pipe. "You need to eat your meat like a good girl. Otherwise you'll miss Washington D.C. and Millicent's engagement party."

Bryony's eyes popped open; the room and her belly sloshed. She reclosed her eyes and swallowed hard. "Millicent's engaged? To Erland Borgstrum?"

"No, to a very nice doctor from Boston."

BANG!

The door slammed against the wall, and Reverend stumbled in, gasping, face red, eyes glazed. He opened his mouth to yell and sank to his knees, grasping his thighs and gasping for air.

"Father!"

As Bryony struggled to sit, lava shot up her throat. She hung over the side of her bed as it hit the floor in splats, while Dr. Gothart, already crouched beside him, inserted a syringe...

She reawakened to darkness, gas lights, and John. The room rocked; her head ached; her stomach quivered; and her heart pounded with frightening speed.

She groped for him, he remained out of reach.

"Hold me, John, I'm so ill."

"Good."

Good?

She burst into tears swiped in his direction. She had to touch a something: shirt sleeve, a trouser leg, something.

But John edged away. "Eat. Your. Meat."

"I will!"

She reached up with two trembling hands, the reach of, not a wife, but of a trusting child. He immediately caught her up in his arms, stroking her hair and murmuring, "There, there, darling, it will be all right."

A tray appeared, the beef soup of Bryony's childhood. John nodded to Trudi, and she brought the bowl to him.

"Give Mrs. Simons the spoon."

Trudi lay it on her palm. Confused, Bryony closed all five fingers around the handle. After Trudi left, Bryony moaned and asked, "Am I...am I to feed myself?"

"You are."

He pushed the hand holding the spoon toward the bowl and into the brown oily liquid. Then he guided the spoon to her mouth. "Why did you alter your diet?"

She swallowed with John monitoring the swallow. "You'll laugh at me."

"I won't."

"Our first...time. I thought... I thought I had meat falling out of me."

John sighed, an actual, troubled sigh, and briefly looked away. "Darling, that's a hymen. Every woman has one. It tears, the first time. That's why it hurts."

She dropped the spoon, splattering broth and intensifying the pounding. "Why did no one tell me this?"

"I don't know."

Tears spilled onto her cheeks and trickled into her mouth. "And now I've killed Father!"

John set the bowl on the nightstand. With his handkerchief, he dabbed her face, he dabbed his waistcoat, he dabbed the bed clothes.

"Your Father isn't 'killed.' He had a mild paroxysm of the heart. He's resting quietly in one of the guest rooms."

"But you two argued so!"

"He'll not fly at me and hinder your freedom."

"He's afraid something bad will happen to me! And now it has!"

"His cage of perverted half-truths has harmed you. Not Chicago. Not New York."

John picked up the bowl and fed Bryony one spoonful after another until all the broth and all the meat pieces were inside her. Her head still hurt, her stomach still felt sick, and her heart still raced.

But at least she felt warm and nourished through and through.

John rose and tucked the blankets around her.

"Eat your meat, Bryony." he said quietly. "We won't repeat this."

She spent the next week in bed reliving the horrible ride home, napping, and eating meat: roasted meat, stewed meat, fricasseed, fried, and doused-in-soup meat, all to the strains of John's persistent and everlasting piano music.

But Bryony understood John's dogged discipline at the keys. John must present nothing less than a flawless performance for the United States president.

She ate beef, chicken, turkey, duck, deer, rabbit, opossum, raccoon, grouse, meat Bryony never dreamed of eating, all served up to her on beautiful bryony-patterned china, a reminder of her place in John's heart.

Sometimes Bryony fed herself; sometimes John fed her. But regardless of how the meat entered her, John supervised every bite. She dared not leave one nibble behind.

As vitality returned, she chastised her foolishness.

Little by little, during their time in New York, the old symptoms had returned, so gradually Bryony scarcely noticed them, especially since Della had scheduled so much winter fun. But Bryony had pushed them aside, confident one good meal of beef steak would restore health and vigor and certain John himself would order it up for her once they settled on the train.

But the meat failed to work immediate magic. She could not compensate for weeks of mistakes in mere days. Somewhere between Jenson and Munsonville, Bryony had fainted.

She had stirred in John's arms to an ax in her head and hooves in her heart as he hurried into Simons Mansion shouting for someone to fetch Dr. Gothart. She closed her eyes against the agony, content to sink into John and blessed blackness.

Vicious shouting between Reverend and John slit the black during her next ascension to the surface, until she gasped awake, like a dying walleye in Mr. Parks' boat.

Then she floundered in a three-cornered net of Dr. Gothart, Bryga, and Howard while a needle and a rubber worm stole her blood.

By the end of the week, Bryony's feeble legs could hold her up. With Trudi grasping her arm, she shuffled down the hall. When Bryony paused to catch her breath, she'd do so near a window, where she yearned to walk along the cobblestone, among the colorful buds poking through the damp earth, and smell the spring air blowing off the lake.

She did not see Reverend. He had already returned to the parsonage to continue his recovery in his own bed.

But Dr. Gothart came. He took her blood pressure, checked her pulse, listened to her heartbeat, pressed her fingernails, and peered into her eyes.

"Well?" John asked.

"She's improving."

But she wasn't.

Although meat enriched Bryony's blood, her mind sagged under the weight of her sins, and her resolve to experience the world withered.

Her father had almost died because she had strayed. And she had almost died because she had strayed from food she needed to live, food her father hated her to eat.

But she needed her father to live. And her father hated the two things that brought life to her life: dead animals and John.

She did not know what to do.

As Bryony read *The Fate of Fenella: by Twenty-four Authors* in the morning room, awash in the golden sunshine and made pleasanter by the tinkling of the piano in the distance, Bryga brought her a stewed bone, on John's orders, Bryga said.

"You're very brave, Mum," Bryga said as she watched Bryony set down the book and reach for the spoon. "I remember when my father fell sick. I was out of my wits with fear I'd lose him. I couldn't leave his bedside, much less travel across the country. I didn't have your trust in modern medicine, which works so many miracles. Why, look at you! Already strong and healthy."

"Did modern medicine save your father, too?"

"No, Mum. He succumbed to his illness."

With a gasp, Bryony gripped the table, but the room still shook, and her mind still raced.

"His heart wasn't strong, you see. I cried for days."

It took half the morning for Bryony to push the contents of her bowl past her trembling lips, but force it she did because she had promised John. She focused her attention on each lowering and raising of her spoon, each opening and closing of her mouth, and each calculated swallow. After that, the soup knew its task and continued on its way without prompting from her: down a throat tight with fear, past her heavy heart, and into a stomach that didn't want it.

When she reached the familiar pink flowers and green vines, signaling the completion of her task, she rang for Trudi.

"Help me back to bed," Bryony said to in answer to the question in Trudi's anxious eyes.

"Yes, Mrs. Simons."

That night, John himself brushed her hair for the first time since they'd come back from New York.

He never spoke except to say, "I love you, Bryony."

She sighed happily and leaned onto his chest, a strong chest where a strong heartbeat with solid love for her. "I love you, too, John."

The next day as they sat in the morning room, John with his coffee and Bryony her tea, John set aside The Times and said, "Our trunks are nearly packed. We leave in the morning."

Bryony calmly took another sip. "I'm not going."

John froze. The look on his face as he looked at her...

Bryony knew she would never forget it. If she lived a hundred years, she would never, ever forget the look on his face.

She'd uttered only three words, but those three words, in the amount of time it took her to say them, severed something between them.

Enough that she almost heard the snap.

Without a word, he rose and stalked across the room, slamming the door behind him.

Soon, the floor reverberated with angry music. Bryony stayed, clutching the chair arms, mind whirling, but resolute.

With Bryga's words rooted in Bryony's heart, Bryony easily held firm.

But she took the rest of her meals that day in bed. She could not risk a relapse; she would not kill her father.

Trudi, not John, readied her for bed that night and brushed her hair.

As Trudi brushed, Bryony's thoughts flew from her hair in bright sparks, the only sounds in the dark and silent room.

Up until their marriage, John had always traveled without her. They had their entire lives together. They would take other trips. They had other opportunities. Surely, with John's enormous talent, he would play the White House again...and probably again.

But if her father died in her absence, something inside Bryony would die. Bryony was not just Mrs. Simons. She was the daughter of Reverend Galien Marseilles. Her daughter parts were older than her wife parts.

And if Bryony died on the road...that, too, would kill her father.

She never felt so desolate.

Long after Trudi had set aside the hairbrush and drawn up the covers, Bryony lay awake, alone. She watched the flames dance on her walls until the fire went out, and then she watched the void, her mind alert and on edge.

She did not hear the door creak open. She did not know John had entered until she felt the mattress sag and heard his plaintive, "Believe, Bryony,"

She melted at the pleading in his voice; she felt the rising of her power, and she turned to find him in the dark.

"Oh, John," she whispered, reaching out to peel the damp strands off his hot forehead and sticky cheeks. "I do believe in us."

And she proceeded to show him just how much, over and over, with her hands as well as her mouth, until dawn's early rays blotted the uneasy darkness, and Bryony sank into eiderdowns of sleep, a soothing warmth of comfort and care, until she bolted up with a fluttering breath and a jolt.

John's side of the bed was empty

The air: oppressively silent without the tinkling of John's piano.

Never minding Trudi or proper dress, Bryony donned a simple salmon-colored gown, forsaking the rest of her finery save for chemise and drawers, and ventured into the quiet hall, looking left and right for signs of John or servants.

On trembling legs, she peered into every room except John's locked room. All empty.

Around the corner, she spied Mildred, dusting a picture frame.

"Has John left?"

"No, Mum."

She slowly took the back stairs, her head swimming, her heart skipping. She passed no one.

Bryony looked all over the first floor, including the guest parlor, the main dining room, John's music room, and John's library.

She only met Robert, dutifully putting away the silver.

"Has John left yet?"

"No. Mrs. Simons."

She carefully inched her way down the basement stairs, praying with every step she didn't pass out, and then astonished the cooks and laundry crew with her appearance in their realm.

The ministering spirits looked up from their washboards, especially distressed.

Bryony waved her hand. "Nothing is wrong. Carry on."

She trudged back upstairs, sick at the silence and the thought of John leaving without saying, "Goodbye." If she lived a thousand years, she would never understand men, especially John.

Where was John? She had checked every room.

Except one.

Bryony straightened her shoulders and raised her head.

She was Mrs. John Simons.

She would go to that room. And if John didn't answer, she would order Bryga to relinquish the key.

Bryony had just reached the main staircase and set her hand on the post when she heard footsteps and voices from the second floor, John conversing with Howard.

As they reached, and then trotted down, the stairs, Bryony felt her world drop, and she clutched the post lest she fall.

He saw her then and paused, briefly, the cold in his eyes colder than any Munsonville winter.

In that moment, Bryony realized her error. Reducing John to pleading hadn't brought them closer. Last night's serene slumber was a laudanum lie.

All the while Bryony had reveled in her openness, John had sowed a thick wall, a non-bryony wall, a wall Bryony knew she'd never scale.

Because he was her husband, John might, maybe, if she was good and only if it suited his purposes, allow her to peer through the cracks from time to time to catch a glimpse of their former future together, but nothing more.

But as Mrs. Simons, the mistress of this household, she couldn't dwell on that now. For she had a more pressing challenge.

She mustn't permit John, let alone the servants, to see just how much his emotional desertion affected her, even when he passed her without a word and strode out the door without a kiss and a backward glance.

Before the Blood, Bryony Simons, Chapter 10: Shades and Shadows

I opened to my beloved; but my beloved had withdrawn himself and was gone: my soul failed when he spake: I sought him, but I could not find him; I called him, but he gave me no answer. (Song of Solomon, Canticle 5:6)

John was gone nearly a month, and not once did he contact her.

But when he returned, she noticed a hunger in his eyes that reminded her of their wedding night. He looked thinner, too, and a bit wan, almost as if he was recovering from a lengthy illness.

During his absence, Bryony had shut herself up in her room, refusing to see anyone except Trudi and Anna, devastated at his desertion, Bryga's deception, and one more loss she had not sufficiently considered at the time.

She had missed the White House!

Bryony cried. And cried. And cried.

Bryony cried until she could cry no more.

By day, Bryony compulsively listened to the music box and picked at her meat, wondering if John even cared if she ate it.

By night, Bryony compulsively listened to her music box and sat at her bedroom window, searching for John's elusive star.

She lost weight. Trudi said so each morning when she came for the breakfast tray still overflowing with food, except for the meat.

Only once did Bryony leave that bed: to take a carriage to visit her father and check on his recovery.

Only once because the coach's rocking made her stomach bounce and her headache.

Only once because she'd put filial devotion before love for her husband.

Only once because she now feared the parsonage.

It happened like this.

On her way to Reverend's office, Bryony had glanced toward the parlor, the place where John proposed to her and wrenched from her father the right to marry her, hoping the memory would comfort her and offer hope.

The portrait Henry had painted hung, as usual, above the mantle.

But with a difference.

The painting itself remained unchanged. It was still a likeness of Bryony' at thirteen, wearing the blue and white checked dress and black pinafore Reverend had selected for the sitting. The wide blue bow still held back her hair, and her child self still smiled back at her, frozen in time, the way Henry saw her.

But since her last visit, someone had artfully positioned candle stubs in front of it, lit candle stubs, with tiny flames.

The candles themselves did not frighten her. The candles were ordinary bluish-white paraffin candles.

But somehow the flames enlivened the eyes, giving the illusion of the child Bryony staring into the soul of the woman.

With the old longcase clock loudly ticking in the background, Bryony tiptoed into the parlor, feeling as if a louder entrance would alert a presence Bryony feared alerting.

Her painted green eyes followed each step.

She stopped, staring at herself. And herself stared back with a frozen smile.

Bryony whirled around, fled to the hall and to the office, where she raised her hand to knock and stopped legs quivering from the effort, fist frozen in midair.

The door was open. The office was empty.

So Bryony, still trembling, tottered to the kitchen where Mrs. Parks was cleaning up from lunch.

"Aunt Bertha, where's Father?"

Mrs. Parks set a plate in the rack to dry. "He's not in the office?"

"No."

"Then he's likely upstairs taking a nap."

"A nap?"

Mrs. Parks looked back at Bryony. "He does that now, sometimes, after the noon meal. And he had a late-night last night." She paused to wipe the corner of her eyes with her apron. "Neta Ashmore delivered a stillborn baby girl."

"Oh, no! How sad! "

"She's torn between returning to Ohio and staying. She might as well stay. Either way, she won't have a man looking after her. At least here she has friends."

"She's very close to the Demars, I know. I'm going to check on Father."

Bryony wobbled to the staircase, fumbling for the furniture as she went lest her legs fail her. She averted her eyes from the parlor and immediately began climbing the creaking stairs, clutching the rail with two hands all the way up.

Her father was napping?

Reverend scorned slothfulness and midday rest and often quoted Proverbs to support his stance: "A little sleep, a little slumber, a little folding of the hands to sleep. So shall thy poverty come as one that travelleth; and thy want as an armed man."

Napping?

Soberly, she reached the top and studied the closed door. Bryony had never crossed this passage; should she now, and if so, should she knock?

But knocking might awaken a man who needed sleep in the early afternoon. She gently set her hand on the knob and turned. The door swung open, and she stepped into the cold gray.

He'd closed the curtains and lit no fire. Well, it was May.

But from the looks of the immaculate hearth, this room had never known fire. Not even in the coldest winters or when the angriest snowstorms blew.

Nor had he pulled back the coverlets on the old straw ticking bed. Instead, he lay on top of them, on his back, hands at his sides, too still for Bryony's liking.

She crept closer.

His chest moved up and down with light breaths, and those came unevenly and far apart. He, too, had lost weight these past weeks. His facial skin sagged, the weight of their deep wrinkles too great to hold it in place. Even in the dim light, Bryony could see his chalky color.

His hair, more white than gray these days but still closely cropped, did a poor job of covering his scalp, which shone bald in random places among the bristly patches.

She, Bryony, had done this to him.

Slowly, she walked downstairs. She heard no noise from the kitchen, a sign Mrs. Parks had finished and gone to prepare dinner for Mr. Parks.

The longcase clock struck twice. Bryony averted any glance to the parlor and with it, her past accusing her.

She slipped into the cloak and softly shut the door behind her.

Jenkins immediately helped her into the carriage.

"All's well?" he asked.

"Yes, thank you."

He closed the door.

Even if John ignored her the rest of her days, she must not further hurt her father. If her health suffered, his would suffer more.

When she returned to Simons Mansion, she ordered steak tartare for dinner and did not go back to bed. Instead, she ate dinner alone in the second-floor dining room.

The next morning, she sent a note of sympathy from her and John to Neta Ashmore.

CP529

By Jennifer Russ

The sharp buzzing echoed throughout the sterile white room and left a ringing in the ears of the woman holding the vibrating saw.

Elbows jutting out in determined angles, her fingers wrapped around the handle as if it were made for them. Brown eyes focused intently behind plastic frames and a soft protective mask covered much of her heart-shaped face. She shook her head, throwing a stray black curl back behind her ear and squared her shoulders in a confident battle stance.

The shrill noise, an everyday occurrence in this room, dulled as it hit the xiphoid process and all resistance was lost. The blade came to a halt at her direction and she placed it aside, returning with a shining set of rib spreaders. They devoured the brittle bones and made a satisfying crack. A smile touched the coroner's face as her big red target came into focus.

Dr. Arrow leaned back, flexed her fingers beneath her protective gloves, and admired the life-giving organ through a set of safety glasses. The potato shaped muscle sat completely still within the chest cavity. Parts of it had paled, due to a lack of blood, and the joining arteries and veins draped like wet noodles over the dead tissue. She expected all of this, of course. The past five years spent in this room had yielded few surprises. In death, all bodies behaved the same.

It was the hearts that made it interesting.

Carefully, she reached into the hollow cove and cupped the organ in her palm. A simple swipe of a scalpel detached the lingering vessels and freed the heart. Beneath the spotlight, she studied all its curves and edges. The lingering blood cleared and revealed the first square patch on the organ. The fabric connected to the tissue with loose thread and the edges fluttered slightly at her exhale.

"Fifteen, maybe twenty years old." She spoke to no one. Another rotation revealed a second patch, this one considerably more worn. "This one is much older; I'd guess around sixty years. Gladys couldn't have been more than twenty."

Gripping the dense organ, she flipped it over to reveal two more patches. One adhered to the tissue perfectly, as if just applied months before death. Dr. Arrow frowned and glanced sideways at the shining table. Amongst her rows of tools sat an opened file folder with Glady's name at the top. She narrowed her eyes, focusing on the loopy handwriting, and quickly nodded.

"Oh, of course. Your husband died six months ago."

The final patch barely hung onto the organ. Dr. Arrow fingered the decaying fabric and squinted at the fading letters stamped upon its surface.

"CP529." Her eyes widened. "This was a prototype patch. You must have been in the first human trials. Incredible."

Her eyes drifted from the heart to the pale blank face just superior to the chest. Deep wrinkles lined the cheeks and two gentle lips receded into a thin line. Long light eyelashes hung heavily upon the closed lids and blanketed the blue caverns beneath. Cheekbones jutted out just enough to showcase the feminine angle to her face and wiry gray hair framed her head like a firm but comfortable pillow.

"What happened to you at such a young age?"

Dr. Arrow placed the heart onto the hanging metal scale and turned back toward the table. She removed her gloves, tossed them into a bin, and flipped through the yellow file folder with purpose. Stopping at a social history form, yellow and brittle from age, she allowed her eyes to linger on two sentences.

"Father and mother died in a car accident. Patient moved to a foster home at age five."

Dr. Arrow sighed and closed the file. She turned and faced the body with slumped shoulders and crossed arms.

"Oh Gladys, I'm so sorry."

Dr. Arrow turned her tape recorder back on and snapped a new pair of gloves onto her hands. She placed the heart back into the body and retrieved the staple gun from her tool table. She spoke as she worked, her voice an exhausted whisper.

"Case 12479, Gladys Vargas. Cause of death has been determined to be a broken heart caused by a faulty first-generation cardiac patch."

Dr. Arrow removed the rip spreader and watched the damaged, yet impressive, organ disappear beneath layers of tissue and bone.

"I will now proceed with closing."

DADDY ATE GRASS

By James Pressler

Today is exciting. Mom puts me in the front seat of the car for the first time. I'm four years old so I'm big now. She doesn't put on my seat belt. She goes back to get Dad, and I jump up and down on the front seat. I like jumping. The front seat is great for jumping, and I don't need to wear a belt here.

Mom comes back to the car with Dad. Dad is being funny. He is running like our dog, Sugar. Mom is holding his belt, and Dad is acting like our dog does when we go for a ride. He is running on his hands and feet, just like Sugar. Mom lets Dad go into the back seat and he curls up. I wave to him. He's being funny today. Mom starts the car and tells me to sit down, but I want to see Dad, so I stand anyway. Mom drives away from the house, and I'm still standing in the front seat so it's okay.

Mom drives fast. Sometimes the car bounces or moves around, and she puts an arm against me to hold me to the seat. She tells me to sit down while she drives, but I want to see Dad because he's funny. He's curled up on our back seat, making growling and barking noises. I wave to him, but he growls and barks like Sugar does when she goes outside. Dad will let Sugar outside then Sugar will eat the long grass by the tree. Then Sugar throws up all the grass and stuff and Dad lets her back in. Dad sounds like that now.

Mom tells me to sit, but I watch Dad. He throws up on the floor of the car just like Sugar does in the backyard.

"Daddy ate grass!" I tell Mom.

I look back at Dad and he looks at me. He looks funny. He doesn't talk. He looks at me, and I look back and laugh. Dad's being funny because he loves me and wants to make me laugh. Mom loves me and lets me ride in the front seat now. This is a great day.

#

I scoop up James and rush him to the car – he's getting heavy for a four-year-old. I put him in the front seat and rush back to the house to get Jerry. An ambulance will take twenty minutes to get here; he doesn't have twenty minutes. He needs to get to the hospital fast. The last time this happened I almost lost him, and he's not dying this time.

He can barely stand on both legs and is bent over from the pain. He's twice my weight but I grab onto his belt and help him stand, then lean him forward and we struggle to the door. He puts out his hands to stop from falling to the ground, his weight driving him forward. I can only aim him toward the car as he stumbles forward, sometimes on all fours. Once he gets in the back seat I'm already around to the front door, keys going to the ignition. It's fifteen minutes to the hospital; he doesn't have fifteen minutes. I put one arm against James bouncing around in the front seat, stomp the gas pedal and pull out of the driveway as fast as that car can move.

This can't happen now; not now. Jerry can't talk from the back seat, he can only groan when he tries to talk. I tell him everything will be okay when I have a few seconds, but there's so much to look out for. Driving so fast, racing every yellow light, rolling through stop signs, there's just no time to stop. I tell James to just sit down, but he's just jumping on the seat. There's no time to belt him in, so I just pin him to the back of the seat with my right arm and pray that everything will be alright.

Where's a cop when you need one? This is an emergency, but there's nobody here to help! Five minutes away, but the traffic's getting worse. Does Jerry have five minutes? I think about faster ways to the hospital while weaving across lanes, looking a block ahead to see if I can make it through the next green light before it turns against me.

Jerry groans loudly, and I hear him throw up. When he got sick in the house, and I saw the blood, I knew his ulcer had torn, but this is so much worse. He has to make it through this.

"Daddy ate grass!" James shouts in excitement from the front seat.

I tell him to sit down, but he's just laughing and there's no time to push him down. I pin him against the back of the seat and spin a hard-right turn. The hospital's in sight. The emergency room entrance looks clear. I stomp the gas and make this final run. This has to work. Nobody is dying today.

#

The moment Carolyn sees me on the floor, bloody vomit all over the carpet, she grabs James and rushes him to the car. I want to stand up, but the pain is crippling. The fire in my gut buckles my whole body, a feeling beyond nausea filling my mind. I know my ulcer is bleeding out, but this is a hundred times worse than last time. I struggle to breathe, and a real feeling hits me. This is how I'm going to die.

Carolyn comes back in the house, yelling for me to get up as she reaches around my waist. I'm twice her weight but with her strength I can rise on weak legs, still bent forward like a three-point stance from my football days. Dragging me by the belt, she pulls me forward and I stumble ahead. Each step is like falling forward, but she won't let me hit the floor. I put out a hand to brace myself against the ground, the other arm wrapped around my gut like it's holding back a volcano. It's an awkward, wobbly trip out the door, but she refuses to stop, even when the pain doubles and I grow dizzy.

She throws me into the back seat like a bag of laundry, and I curl up as tight as my muscles allow. The fire in my gut is white-hot and radiating into my chest. I'm growing light-headed, and my toes and fingers start to tingle. I know this is death creeping in, and the fear makes me fight harder to just stay awake.

Each turn of the car rolls me around in the back seat, the dizzying motions making my nausea worse. I try to tell Carolyn to be careful, but only pained moans come out. I can hear the boy laughing above me, and Carolyn telling him to sit down. It sounds so distant, like they're both at the end of a tunnel, drifting away from me. I want to tell them both that I love them before I die, but I can only groan, the effort to even say a word choking in my throat.

As the fire in my gut boils over, my whole body contracts and I throw up on the floor. The odor of bile and blood fill my nose, but the release eases my pain. My hands and feet grow numb, my dizziness now a warm sensation of floating, drifting away like an afternoon nap. So this is what the end feels like.

"Daddy ate grass!" James shouts from above me.

I look up at the boy, my face growing warm as the pain drifts away and the warmth of a thick down comforter runs up my arms and legs. I know I am fading away. I see him laughing, looking down at me with a look of joy. I love my family, and I won't leave them until I have to. I focus on his little round head, on his happy face. As long as I see that face and hear his laughter, I'm still alive. As long as I can, I will stay with them.

DELETED SCENE

R. Michael Markley

Author's note: This scene did not make it in the final edit of my novel "Necessary Death." My editor felt it wasn't needed to move the story along. I have chosen to resurrect it from the cutting room floor to share it in this anthology. So what you are reading is like a deleted scene. Perhaps it will entice you to purchase the whole book. Enjoy!

The Hidden Agenda was packed. The music playing loud from the jukebox, with the cigarette smoke hanging like a heavy fog. Like most bars, lights were dim, even if it was mid-day, it could be mistaken for late at night. Luther promised Dominic he had a lead. Tonight they would finally be able to meet.

Big Jacks stood behind the bar serving up anything to those who needed to wash down all the world has to offer with whatever would ease the pain. In the corner, a very thin, hollowed-eye person sat lighting a cigarette with the end of the one he had just finished. His hair was long, stringy, and greasy. He looked to be in his late forties. When he saw Luther, he got up almost running to Luther.

He grabbed at Luther's sleeve. "Sit here." Brushing off the chair while pushing Luther into it. Luther couldn't believe that someone so skinny could have so much strength. The little man took the chair across from him surveying the room. He held out his grubby hand. "My name is Spider. If you got what I need, I got what you want."

Luther refused the handshake but noticed that Spider didn't have a thumb on his right hand. Luther sat there a moment starring at Spider. "Have we met before?"

Spider had the shakes; he needed a fix. He didn't even seem to hear Luther's question. That's okay Luther thought, he would get what he wanted without giving anything up. Spider fidgeted watching Luther with every move. Luther, on the other hand, scanned the crowd of the Hidden Agenda. He wanted to ensure that he was not being watched. He wanted no ties to this little snitch, just information.

Spider's shaking increased. "I pick up bits of information from everyone just by listening to their conversations from the shadows. No matter what it is, it gets caught in my web. That's how I got the name Spider."

All of a sudden Spiders attention turned from his shakes to the girl playing pool. "Look, look, look." he pointed. "See, see, see?"

Luther looked over at the pool table; there a couple was playing pool. He remained silent.

"Right there, right there, right there." Again Spider pointed. "That is a fine woman right there, yes sir, mighty fine."

The woman stood about five feet tall with blonde hair, wearing very heavy eyeliner with bright red lipstick. Her skirt being way too short, she also wore thigh high boots. She looked too old to be dressing like that. But for her profession, more than appropriate. Spider started talking too fast for Luther to comprehend.

"She, she, she is a fine woman, just look at those legs and those lips. Oooh weee!" Spider shouted loud enough making the couple looked over in their direction.

"Shut up you little..." Luther started.

"Shhh!" Spider interrupted. "Don't talk so loud, they can hear us."

Luther kept feeling that he might be the one getting played. "So who is she?"

"She is fine; that's who she is."

"You've said that more than once, what's her name?"

"That my friend is Joy."

"I don't care what she may or may not have brought you. All I want to know is her name."

"That's what I am telling you man, her name is Joy. And she may or may not have brought me some. That's none of your business. But I'll bet if you ask her, she would be happy to bring..."

Luther gave Spider a narrowed look. What is it you got for me you little rat? and what's the big deal about her?"

"Relax, relax, relax," Spider whispered.

Spider searched the pockets of his army jacket. Luther started to not only get impatient but also repulsed by the smell hanging around Spider. The more Luther studied Spider the more he knew he looked like someone from Luther's past. Then it hit him. Ray Welleden, the high school football star and all-state linebacker. A ladies' man in school, all the girls acted as if Elvis just walked in the room whenever Ray did. That's why he so easily pushed Luther into his seat. Though he was as thin as a rail he still knew how to use his body weight to move people.

"That little Joy right there," Spider started. "She is in bed with a cop. That cop's name is Mark Capwell. Joy is going around saying this cop is making her life miserable and there is nothing she can do about it. She says he's bragging how he's helping to blow this city wide open with a blood bath. That he helped take out this guy they call Rhino."

Luther clenched his teeth. "What makes you so sure?"

"Well the other night, I had some good stuff, so I shared it with Joy. So she shared with me, if you know what I mean. She opened up telling me how this cop taking is taking advantage of her. She told me that this Capwell had a lot of stuff on her, so if she ever said anything, he can make sure she would never be found. Sounds like she may have something that you want. I know she has something I want."

"Shut up you little worm," Luther whispered.

"Look you asked me to ask around, I gave you what I heard. Now it's your turn."

"Have you told this to anyone else?"

"Nope, no one cares about the problems of a streetwalker."

Luther straightened up looking over at Joy. "Does anyone else know we're meeting?"

"I don't share my business transactions with nobody. The less people know the less they will get hurt or I will get caught. Got it? Now what do you have for me?"

Luther thought for a moment, Spider's right. No one would care about a streetwalker just like they wouldn't care about a junkie. He would wait long enough for people to forget about this little termite, coming to the conclusion another junkie died. But he would get with Joy tonight. Luther stood up.

44

Spider panicked, he stood in Luther's path blocking his exit. "Where, where, where ya going big guy?"

"Look, Ray, you may have been able to stop me in high school, but the years have taken their toll. The drugs have also done a job on you. Don't make me hurt you. I'm going to leave. I will call you in a couple of days. Don't worry; you will be glad that you waited. But until then get out of my way."

Spider cowered and backed away in shame that Luther recognized him. He stepped aside and Luther passed. As he did, Spider grabbed Luther by the arm whispering, "Don't forget man, you owe me."

Luther stopped, starring straight into Spider's eyes, "Don't threaten me. You don't want to get tangled up with me. I will squash you like the bug that you are. No one will ever miss you. Like you said, no one cares about a streetwalker; well, no one cares about a junkie either."

Spider froze. He didn't move a muscle until Luther was completely out of site. He sat down trying to smile while he stared at Joy.

When Luther left The Hidden Agenda, he called Dominic.

"What have you got?" Luther heard on the opposite end of his phone.

Luther knew Dominic would be waiting for his call not being surprised at all by this greeting. "I know who's responsible for your brother's death." Luther answered all of Dominic's questions. Before hanging up he assured Dominic. "Trust me, they're going to pay for what they did to your brother. "I guarantee it." Luther closed his phone.

DEVOTION NUMBER ONE

By Dale Hansen

WEEK 1   **Genesis 1:1-2:4**   **Focus: 2:3**

Overview: Genesis tells of God creating this world. He created the lights, the waters, the land, the plants, the trees, the animals and the stars. This took Him six days, and He rested on the seventh day.

Focus: God made everything in nature for us and Himself to enjoy. We see many varieties of plants, flowers, birds and animals. He then rested from His creation on the seventh day (2:3). He decided this day would be holy and set apart and this day would have its own commandment: "Remember to observe the Sabbath day by keeping it holy" (Exodus 20:8).

How to Apply: Have you ever scheduled some rest time into your schedule? Have you ever put a big R on a day on your calendar? During this week, do one or more from this list:

- walk in the park.
- read a book.
- go to a movie with a friend.
- take a nap.
- start a book of the Bible.

One of my favorites things to do is when I am outside at night and I look up for the moon. I am always thanking our great God for the beauty of the moon when the sky is clear, and the moon is full. A less than full moon will reveal the stars in the night sky as a reminder of how awesome God is. The moon is still there when it is cloudy. God is still with us on cloudy and difficult days.

(His first chapter in his second book. "Journey through the Old Testament".)

DEVOTION NUMBER TWO

By Dale Hansen

WEEK 52   **Malachi 3:1-18**   **Focus: 3:6**

Overview: The final voice of the Old Testament is a book written by Malachi. Four hundred years would pass before we hear from John the Baptist (3:1). Malachi's message includes the Jews are still not completely following God. Again, God offers repentance (3:6-7) and a promise of mercy (3:17-18). Malachi tells the future where God will return and bring judgement on all those who deny Him.

Focus: Are you ready for His return? Do you need to return to Him first? Our spiritual growth to deepen our relationship with Him is a steady progression with ongoing adjustments in our lives. Disobedience will result in consequences and judgment.

How to Apply: During this week, evaluate your time usage to stay on course as listed below:

- Time in His Word.
- Time with your family.
- Time and commitment to church.
- Time on your computer/ I-pad/ cell phone.
- Time working on relationships–family & friends.

I checked the APPs on my phone and reduced the number. The biggest time waster for me was the ESPN APP. It has been deleted. Pick one of the above for this week. Or delete an APP!

(His last chapter in his second book. "Journey through the Old Testament".)

DRIVING IN ITALY

By Robert Hafey

Driving in any country other than your own can be adventuresome and occasionally problematic. As proof, the left side mirror on almost every rental car in Ireland is either missing or broken and dangling from the side of the car for a good reason.

I have had the opportunity to drive in many countries but driving in Italy, the home of the Ferrari and Lamborghini, created some lasting travel memories. This may be the case because I and many of the local drivers envision ourselves as Mario Andretti piloting an iconic hand-built Italian sports car. In reality, we are driving dinky little four-cylinder diesel vehicles like the Fiat Punto.

On our first trip to Italy we decided to use only trains to travel between the large cities on our itinerary. We based that decision on multiple facts. The first being we would not need a car when visiting the larger cities. Having to find parking, and possible pay for it, before we urban hiked around those cities seemed like a waste of time and money.

The driving learning curve also influenced our decision. Driving is like riding a bike. Once someone learns how they should be able to jump into any car and just head on down the road anywhere in the world. But there are different driving rules, road signs and customs in every country. Therefore, the uncertainty encountered while learning by doing can be challenging and stressful.

The one exception to our train transportation decision was to rent a vehicle for our four-day stay in Tuscan wine country. Consequently, on our last day in Florence, we walked, while our suitcases clickety-clacked as they bounced across a sunny stone-covered plaza, to a nearby car rental facility.

When it was our turn, we approached the counter and said, "Buongiorno." Our customer service agent, based on that one spoken word, determined our country of origin and began to speak English with a lovely Italian accent.

While completing the required paperwork she asked, "Would you like to rent a GPS unit?"

I replied, "No, I have a Garmin GPS."

With a twinkle in her dark Italian eyes she responded, "Oh, you already have a marriage saver."

As we drove away in our small gray standard transmission Fiat Punto we chuckle because we knew, from our own past experience, the customer service agent was right.

We put the address of our Tuscan agriturismo (bed and breakfast) into our GPS unit and drove off toward our countryside lodging. As the Garmin barked out orders to turn left or right, we obeyed without emotion.

Our agriturismo was located in the middle of wine country. Rolling hills covered with vineyards surrounded our accommodations. It was a laid back, quiet and peaceful setting when compared to Rome and Florence. We filled our afternoons by relaxing there but each morning we excitedly piled into the Punto after breakfast and drove off to visit and explore a different Tuscan hill town.

Unlike the straight and flat roads at home in the Midwest the narrow lanes in Tuscany constantly twisted and turned as they directed us to and around the ancient hill towns. I had anticipated driving in Italy for I knew the roads would be curvy. I had once owned a Triumph Spitfire, a small British two-seat sports car. I fondly recalled the fun I had guiding that car around curves as I now ran through the gears of my Punto, then down shifting at each bend in the road before accelerating while coming out of the curve's apex.

Passing another car safely seemed impossible because I rarely encountered a straight section of road. Not that I wanted to pass anyone. But every Italian driver, familiar with the local roadways, wanted desperately to pass me. Looking in my rear-view mirror I could see them twitching, like Formula 1 drivers, as they rode my ass while waiting for the perfect opportunity to pass, which was never going to happen.

To support their machismo, I became an expert at pulling over and letting them zoom by. At first, I thought they were waving hello as they passed, but soon realized it was some other kind of gesture involving their fingers.

I asked my wife, "Do you think there is an app that translates Italian hand gestures?"

Our reliance and trust in the GPS unit, during our four days in Tuscany, prevented the, "I told you to turn there, but you never listen to me!" conversations that often occurred during our pre-GPS ownership days. Trust can be a fragile thing.

One afternoon, when returning to the agritourismo on a familiar road she, the GPS unit, instructed us to take a right turn onto a very small road. Since the unit was programmed to always take the quickest route, we extended trust, assumed she knew a shortcut and took the right turn. Quickly the road turned to gravel and then tree branches began to brush both sides of the car. Soon it sounded exactly like we were driving through a waterless automated car wash.

I stopped, put the Punto in reverse, and backed off the hiking trail while my wife yelled at the Garmin as if she was talking to me.

"What were you thinking?" I could tell that wasn't a good road to turn on. Do I have to give you directions?"

As she continued to lay into the Garmin, I mumbled to myself, "I am falling in love with that Garmin."

On another trip to Italy we flew into Rome. After clearing customs and retrieving our bags we made our way to the car rental facility. After twenty minutes I began mumbling complaints under my breath about the seemingly disorganized facility and staff. Only after I noticed someone with a numbered card in their hand, did I realize I was supposed to take a number and wait until I was called to the counter. That provided a chance for some self-flagellation using Italian words. Deficiente, Idiota!

Anyone looking at me could see I really needed to sleep and had entered the "zombie state" by the time we completed the paperwork and were escorted to our Fiat Punto. We climbed into the diminutive car and loaded our first destination, Castiglioncello, into our GPS unit. To get to this small seaside town on the Ligurian Sea, we would have to drive three and a half hours north of Rome. We planned to spend two nights in that coastal city before driving almost directly east to Siena, where we would spend time with friends at a large villa.

Near the airport we found the entrance ramp for a northbound expressway and within minutes I had the Punto cruising along at ninety kilometers an hour. Discounting the four and a half minutes of restless sleep I had on the flight over, I had now been awake for about twenty-two hours. Not yet dead tired, but getting close, I focused on the drive.

Then about an hour into our trip, when a toll booth appeared ahead, I panicked and swerved back and forth between the electronic pass and cash lanes. My mind started racing like the Punto's engine. Where to go? Did the rental car have a transponder? Do I have enough cash?

I chose a cash lane. Rather than an attendant greeting me with a "buongiorno" and an offer to help I found myself staring at an ATM machine. Great I thought. Then I notice the universal symbols of money transactions, the Visa and MasterCard logos next to a slot.

I pulled a credit card from my wallet and inserted it while praying I was not turning over my financial information to the mafia. I pressed what I thought might be the appropriate keys and waited for the toll gate to open. It did! Feeling confidently experienced, I headed down the tollway hoping more toll booths appeared on the horizon.

The adrenaline rush resulting from that toll booth experience jolted me into a wide-awake state for at least thirty minutes. But soon after we both hit a wall and agreed we needed a dose of caffeine.

I pulled off at the next gas station rest stop area. As I wobbled in the Italians knew exactly what I needed before I opened my mouth to say, "Due expresso." While one took my payment, another cranked up the gleaming stainless-steel steam driven coffee extraction machine. After a few hisses and puffs of steam the barista turned to me holding two diminutive plastic cups. The blackest of viscous liquids filled them about a third of the way up. Gently gripping each one between a thumb and index finger I walked back to the car.

Upon seeing me holding two large thimbles my wife asked, "Where is the coffee?" I just smiled and handed her a thimble. We toasted our good fortune before drinking the expresso like a petite shot of whiskey. Within minutes caffeine pulsated through my veins and we safely continued our road trip to Castiglioncello.

After two lovely days in that coastal city we departed for the sixty-six-mile trip east to Siena. The time to travel any distance in Italy, if not on a four-lane expressway, is always double the time it takes in the Midwest. The reason is simple, a mountainous and hilly landscape. After two hours of travel we approached the area of the villa and could see the local terrain was made up of large plowed hills.

Exiting the expressway, we followed a small meandering road to the villa entrance located at the base of a large hill. A sharp left and a climb up a long steeply angled driveway would take us to the buildings visible far above. I put the standard transmission in first gear and gunned it. Up we went. I felt pretty cocky about my manual transmission skills as the engine raced and we continued our ascent. Then a closed automatic gate, blocking our entrance, appeared just before we crested the hill.

While using some of the choice Italian swear words I had memorized, I jammed in the clutch and stood on the brake pedal to keep us from rolling backwards uncontrollably down the steep hill. My wife, intent on saving her own life, exited the vehicle to open the gate. As I sat there swearing in Italian, I realized I would have to rely on the clutch popping skills I had acquired during my late teen years. While revving the engine like the driver of a dragster about to rocket down a quarter mile track, I quickly let out the clutch and zoomed to the top. It was an adrenaline rush. I could not wait to leave the villa so I could drive back up that hill.

On one of the days at the villa, everyone jumped into a car and we all drove into Siena for the weekly morning market. I had driven into Siena a few days earlier and knew the entire day could be spent driving in circles looking for parking. Today was no different, town was jammed with cars and locating a parking spot would be as difficult as finding deep dish pizza in Italy. We observed and then decided to follow signs to a parking area adjacent to the local soccer stadium. After parking we made our way to what might be considered an event akin to a traveling circus.

This outdoor traveling market, set up and taken down every day, moved from town to town. For the next few hours we mingled with the locals as we wandered past stalls, tents and trailers containing meat, cheese, wine, clothing, shoes, housewares and souvenirs.

When we had seen enough, we walked to city center to meet up with friends from the villa for lunch. After lunch, as we headed back toward the soccer stadium parking area, we noticed the market stalls, trailers, tents, and all of the merchandize they had contained, had been removed. Only multiple cleaning crews, sweeping up debris and removing trash, remained in the market area as we passed.

We located our car and five of us jumped in. As we drove toward the exit I commented, "This is a different gate from the one we entered this morning." As soon as I exited, I wondered why there were no other cars and quickly realized no traffic was allowed in the market area at this time.

I sped up while frantically looking for a way out. One of the smart-ass back seat drivers kindly pointed out, "That was the wrong exit."

Soon we sighted a gated exit. I pulled up to the gate and nothing happened. Another back-seat driver suggested, "A few Hail Mary's might help." "Ha-ha," I responded.

I backed up and parked the car. I instructed my passengers to stay put while I ran back and asked someone how to get out.

Finding a cleaning crew, I did my best to explain the situation using hand gestures and grimaces. In response I believe they said, "Pulla upa toa agata." Figuring I had not pulled in far enough to trip the gate sensor, I ran back, hopped in and pulled up until the front of the car was in contact with the gate. No luck. I backed up and drove off seeking another escape route.

On our first trip to the automated gate I had viewed vehicle traffic moving at the far end of a street we passed. The only problem, it was a one-way street. Since the street was devoid of traffic, I made a snap decision while shouting, "Hang on," and raced down the street going the wrong way.

Cleaning crews shouted loudly and made animated hand gestures as we sped past them. While I screamed to my passengers, "Do not make eye contact," to prevent any feelings of guilt, I raced to the end of the street and just barely squeezed the car between two metal posts, intended to block vehicles, in order to enter the flow of traffic. We had escaped.

I demanded silence in the car while listening for the sound of sirens. The only sound heard was that of the wind whistling through the car windows.

Feeling euphoric I shouted, "How about that for some fun," which caused joyous laughter that continued all the way back to the villa.

It was revealed, shortly after our return, that someone in the back seat had videoed the escape sequence using their cell phone. Later as I snuck out the front door of the villa to inspect both sides of the rental car for damage, I could hear hearty wine infused laughter ricocheting through the Tuscan hills as everyone watched the video multiple times.

For the balance of the trip, the now immortalized phrase, "Do not make eye contact," was used even when it was inappropriate. This confirmed my belief that only adversity creates lasting travel memories and stories.

I long to hear the stories associated with all of the Irish rental cars that have a missing or dangling left side mirror. Having to drive in the left lane, while sitting on the right side of the car, is exactly why you should drive in Ireland. The opportunity to create a lasting travel story exists at every turn in the road. Just remember, do not to make eye contact with the attendant when returning the rental car.

GONE TOO FAR

R. Michael Markley

One of our writer's group prestige's leaders gave us a prompt to create whatever came to our mind. A poem, short story, song or dance. (Which actually happened). To this prompt: **A baby cheetah shows up at your door, asking for a sandwich.** *This was my contribution.*

The smoke hung so thick I waited for a foghorn to belch at any second. Instead I heard the familiar repeating cough that began the anthem to pot smokers everywhere. My brother-in-law was having his annual Halloween party which meant plenty of weed, alcohol and rock and roll! The song "Sweet Leaf" was escaping from his speakers at a volume that most adults would say could be damaging to our ears. Little did they know, we knew this; we just didn't care. One of our many rebellious antics that made us feel in control. The adults, they didn't even call it music so why would we care what they thought about volume.

Michelle sat next to me with her hand on my leg. She handed me a joint, encouraging me to take another hit. I obliged. The rhythm of the music increased along with the volume now making it difficult to carry on a conversation. But who talked? The smoke being highlighted along with the neon felt posters taking up space on the walls. The black light made everything appear to be glowing. With the alcohol, the drugs, the rock and roll it made the atmosphere surreal. The only thing missing, the sex.

Sitting across from me in a white top hat, tails, shoes, holding on to a cane was a good friend of my brother-in-law named Chris. His character for Halloween was Alice Cooper. Alice wore that same outfit while performing his "Welcome to My Nightmare" tour. Well with the effect of the black light on his all white suit, the effect of the drugs on my already numbed conscience I would have sworn on a stack of Bibles Mr. Cooper sat right across from me.

Another beer, another toke. The room now intoxicated with music. The floor of the basement now packed with partygoers. Dancing, laughing, to the beat. Michelle grabbed my hand. "Come on," she yelled. "Let's dance."

"I can't dance," I protested.

"Shut up man. You can at least do the bump. That's easy"

I proceeded to bump to the beat of the song. Before I knew it, I was in the middle of the floor with all the other happy people just having a great time.

Time. It seems to stand still while you party. The problem is it doesn't. Before you know what hit you, it's past midnight the music has stopped and it's just you with a couple of friends sitting around trying to stop the craving for food. I sat there starring at my yellow stained fingers wondering where the golden, orangish color came from.

"They're a pain, I hate eating Cheetos. I can never get my fingers clean" Michelle shared as she sucked on her fingers trying to erase the stain.

I had a hard time understanding her. Was it the music? Maybe the drugs? Maybe both.

I knew it had gone too far when Alice, I mean Chris came into the room shouting and laughing hysterically "There's a baby Cheetah at the door asking for a sandwich."

"What did you say?"

"There's a baby Cheetah at the door asking for a sandwich."

"That's what I thought you said. I got to see this, show me." I pushed myself past Chris running up the stairs taking two at a time. I had to see this. I headed toward the front door. When I opened it, Andy was standing there. I turned toward Chris.

"This isn't a Cheetah, that's Andy."

Both of them started to laugh uncontrollably. "What are you talking about Mike?"

"Chris came downstairs telling us there's a baby Cheetah at the door asking for a sandwich."

Chris yelled out. "I didn't say that. I said, "Maybe we should get rid of the Cheetos off the floor before Andy's wife turns into a witch."

I stood there comatose. I could have sworn I heard there's a baby Cheetah at the door asking for a sandwich. I knew then I had gone too far. I just sat there while my fingers turned even more yellow as I finished the bag of Cheetos.

GOOD FORTUNE

By Ryan M. Harris

Sivia was terrified. Only a month into her new marriage and it didn't look like it was going to last much longer. She stood trying to figure out something better to do then watch helplessly. Behind her back she fingered the guard of her sword, knowing full well the weapon would do her no good here. While there were very few problems she couldn't solve with a sword; one of those problems was her mother.

Her mother had ruined her first marriage. As a younger girl she'd married a Goblin warrior named Elkbleed. Sivia was a half blood, half goblin, half human, and she'd missed both races definition of beauty by a wide margin. To humans she was too muscular for a female, too boney in the face, and the olive tone of her skin was offsetting if not disturbing. To goblins she was too pale, and not having a single wart was a deformity. So when she met Elkbleed and he took a liking to her she counted herself lucky. He was a catch: a vicious killer, fantastic with an axe, and fast on his way to ruling his own clan. When she'd brought him to meet her parents, she was certain they'd approve. Instead, Mother bit his nose off, before he even got in door. Elkbleed had run off into the woods, hands clutched over his face, trying to keep the juices in, and crying.

Mother had watched him go, still chewing, a smug grin on her face, and blood running down her many chins. Sivia never saw Elkbleed again; no one did, that she knew of. The whole thing had been horrifying.

If they'd had anywhere else to go, she'd have never brought Gerstan home. As it was, she was starting think they should have stayed and fought the knights.

They stood on the doorstep of her parent's home: a mud brick cottage built deep in the Olkam forest. It was dark out with a kind of blue tint to everything. Outside the forest it might have been a sunny day, but under the ancient and tight weaved canopy of the Olkam it was always some shade of dark.

Gerstan was shaking.

He was a human, and a skinny one at that, weighing less than a hundred fifty pounds with his armor on, spread out over a tall lanky frame. His skin was so pale it nearly glowed in the dark. His red hair was sweaty and tangled. They'd been running for a day and a half straight. They were both exhausted, and filthy.

Mother was walking around him, chortling to herself: a noise reminiscent of bovine. Like Gerstan, she was human, but at six foot seven and more than four hundred pounds she looked more like an ogre, with stringy black hair tied back through opossum skulls, and a mad look in her eye that came from nearly a hundred years of cannibalism.

As mother passed behind him, Gerstan gave her a pleading 'help me' look. Sivia tried to imply back with her eyes: Run and I'll follow! Saying it out loud would certainly have meant one of mother's meaty fists crushing his skull.

Gerstan wasn't running. Mother stopped in front of him.

"You're stringy!" The old woman screamed at him. "But, are you a stringy turkey, chicken, or piglet?"

"Mother if you -"

"Shut up girl!" Her mother commanded.

Sivia shut up; her mother still scared her.

Mother turned back to Gerstan and held her hand up in front of his chest, palm out. Mother's eyes closed, and she stood there for a moment unmoving. Then her hand began to quiver. The muscles in her arms, normally hidden beneath the many layers of blubbery fat, strained and became visible like she was pushing against something very heavy.

If she kills him, Sivia promised herself, I'll slit my throat right here and show the old bag what she's done.

Mother stepped back, her hand dropping as though whatever she'd been pushing against had knocked her back. Her eyes opened, staring Gerstan in the face. "He can stay," she grumbled, "but no shitting on the furniture, boy!"

"No Ma'am," Gerstan stuttered. He now looked confused in addition to frightened.

Mother growled in a low tone, her lips curling up to show her teeth, then she lumbered off into the house, mumbling as she went.

It was a better judgment then Sivia had hoped for. It seemed Gerstan would even be allowed inside the house.

Her old room was a shrine to her early childhood, or a picturesque fantasy of it. The place had never been this neat when she lived here. Her toys covered the shelves, carefully aligned, dusted, and polished to perfection. None of the furniture had been moved an inch. Even her old quilt, albeit with many of its patches repaired, was draped over the bed's footboards, clean and folded as though her twelve-year-old self might want it any moment.

Gerstan sat on the edge of the bed. His hands still shaking as he emptied his bags.

"What about your father?" he asked.

She envied women who could say they fathers were all gruff. "Let's worry about one problem at a time."

Bending over at the waist she shook off her chain mail. Sweat had pasted the gambeson underneath to her skin. Painfully, she had to peel it free. Now naked from the waist up, she glanced over at Gerstan. He was stacking his wicker cages on the nightstand and paying no attention to her. She'd scolded him a while back about gawking at her tits every time she changed clothes; of course, she hadn't really wanted him to stop.

She hurried to undo her greaves, then kicked off her boots and shook out sore legs. She set her sword on a weapons rack she'd made for her first knife when she was eight, and free of her armaments slid onto the bed beside Gerstan.

"I think we should head out tonight," He said without looking up.

Sivia frowned. Now that she knew her mother wasn't going to kill him, she was starting to look forward to weekend with a real bed. They'd yet to have any sort of a honeymoon.

"Are you that scared of my father?"

"Yea, actually. But, I'm more worried about bringing law to his door, and getting his daughter hung in the front yard."

He pulled a piece of moldy bread from his pocket, crumbling it up to feed his tiny prisoners. Most of the cages were empty. He was down to only three fairies, having had to use several against their pursuers. He had a male forest fairy, a red mountain female, and a cave female. He'd been so happy to find the cave one. Gerstan collected fairies, having found a variety of cruel uses for them, and rare specimens excited him.

They looked like humans after he cut their wings off, except at a hundredth the size, and with neon skin. They were cute in a way, like cowering dolls.

Gerstan rationed out the breadcrumbs.

"Seems a silly time to panic," Sivia said worming her way behind him so she could rub his shoulders. "Correct me if I'm wrong, but we made it."

"I don't make it," Gerstan said shaking his head. "I get caught. There's some rule to the world that says the good guys will always win, and that I'll never, ever have a plan that works out."

"This was our plan." She raked her knuckles down his ribs. "I'll bite you." She kissed him under the ear, letting her teeth graze him.

"I'd rather you didn't."

"Then quit worrying. I'm sick of worrying; we lost them, and... we're wasting time in which we have a bed."

"Oh?"

"Yea," She whispered, breathing heavily on him. "We've a while before dinner, and we could spend it worrying or...we could count all our money!"

Gerstan grinned. The money pouch sat beside him on the pillows. They hadn't dared do much more then open it in the brush. He looked at it, then back at her. She challenged him with an arch of her eyebrows.

They both dove after it, slapping and kicking at each other like two greedy children fighting over a toy. Gerstan was closer and got a hold of it first. Blocking her with his shoulder and a hand in her face, he was starting to open it when she changed strategies. Giving up on reaching the bag by going over top of him, she went around and put him in a choke hold.

"Uckk," he choked, "honey...ack"

He now had to devote both his hands to pulling her elbow away from his throat so he could breath.

"Give me the bag!" She demanded.

Gerstan threw himself backward taking her with him. She hit her head and shoulders on the wall. The impact broke the shelf above them, and it fell, boards and wooden animals raining down on them.

He conceded first. "Truce," he managed to say under her grip.

"Truce," she agreed, letting go of his neck to rub her head.

With one hand each on the bag they dumped it between them, and then stared down at its contents in slack-jaw reverie. It was the most money she'd ever seen in one place, more money than all the fortunes her father had ever gained and lost in his whole long life of scheming. They were solid gold marks of the realm. Their value aside they were almost pieces of art, cast with the Artemian seal on one side: a compass devoid of the direction south. From the other a relief of the king smiled, which was sort of funny considering they'd killed his son to get it.

Sivia picked up a handful of the coins and let them slip through her fingers. They were heavier than they looked. Gerstan had a smile ear to ear. He was smearing the pile flat. Then he scooped it back up and started again. She lobbed a coin at him; bouncing it of his forehead. He threw a handful of them back at her. She shielded her face with her arm and a few of the cold things went sliding down her shirt.

She shrieked, and Gerstan laughed at her. Growling playfully at the insult she tackled him, knocking him to his back. She pinned his arms down above his head. Too competitive for his own good Gerstan strained against her trying to get up.

Dipping down she licked him on the cheek, moving back quickly before he decided to head-butt her.

"Yuck." She stuck her tongue out at him. "You need a bath."

#

He quit struggling and she let go of his arms. His efforts turned to the leather ties that kept her pants up. While he worked, she picked up scattered coins and built a pile on his chest. Little kings smiled up at her

Father had aged a lot since she'd left. He'd shrunk at least a foot in height. Sitting in his chair, he could barely see over the table. His skin had turned brown, or as he explained it: his spots were connecting. A hundred and five was an unheard-of age for a goblin, a race whose doctors determined the health of their elderly by throwing stones at them to see if they could still move fast enough dodge. But Father wasn't a normal goblin. Even in his youth he'd preferred study over fighting and stranger still his sharp mind and desire to learn had earned him the respect of other races. Even the elves of black kettle hill had once let him into their library, though they watched over him swords in hand. Now, he was both feared and respected by all the Goblinac clans. They thought him a sorcerer who could turn a man into kindling wood with little effort. It would take a very brave doctor to throw a rock at him.

Though, Sivia had never actually seen him do anything more arcane then read.

"What color were their uniforms?" Father asked, peering up from a scroll that charted the various local coat-of arms. His plate of food was growing cold on the table in front of him.

"Most wore blue with white or yellow markings in all different patterns. There were a few others leading them, dressed in snot green with darker green stripes. They had short bows instead of shields."

Seated across from her, Gerstan frowned and fidgeted in his seat. Digging into the collar of his tunic he produced one of their gold coins.

She had to clamp her hand over her mouth to keep from laughing. In the sudden effort to be silent she choked on a piece of meat and after gagging and having to cough it up, she ended up making more noise than if she'd just laughed.

"You forget how to chew, girl?" Father snapped, he sat his scroll down to peer at her, his eyes looking huge behind his spectacles. Father hated to be interrupted while he was trying to look intelligent. That of course went double for having to impress his new son-in-law.

"Sorry," she got out, draining her ale, tears streaming down her face.

"The greens are Cason Rangers, local band of bandits and

poachers."

Father rolled his scroll up, setting it aside, and pulled another from his pile. He mumbled under his breath as he searched the new one. "Nothing fits the others exactly, single color but not being uniform; my best guess is your others are Artemian guard, personal militia of the noble families. If they're together they've either been conscripted by royalty or the nobles actually agreed on something…"

Father gave her a hard look; his features wrinkled at the corners, and the hide atop his nose scrunched up making his moles move. "Either way those would have to be some very angry Artemians."

Sivia swallowed hard then got up to refill her glass.

"There was another man with them," Gerstan said. The coin in his fingers disappeared with a coin trick disguised as him reaching for his fork. "He was wearing all white, and carried a wooden sword like a child's toy, no armor, no other weapons."

"Sounds like a fool to me," Mother grunted looking up from her food for the first time. Gravy and debris of chicken was smeared across her face.

"I think he was in charge of the whole group," Gerstan said. "Could just be some crazy captain. But he was riding front most of the way, and I got a pretty good look at them crossing the river. Something about the way he carried himself worries me a little. I'd like to know if he's someone important."

"Important?" Father's leaned onto the table to glare at Gerstan. "What have gotten my little girl into, boy, that important people are chasing you?"

"Couldn't say sir," Gerstan replied doing a good job of sounding genuinely ignorant. "Maybe they're after someone else and got after us by mistake."

"Humph," Father grumbled, settling back in his chair. "I know you're lying to me you little shit! And I'll tell you, neither of you is leaving until I find out how much trouble you've gotten her into! Lots of people owe me favors and I'll find out."

"Quit threatening them Ural!" Mother snarled, slamming her fist down and shaking everything on the table. "You'll scare them off and they'll never bring the grandchildren to visit us."

"You're the one who -" Father started.

Mother jumped from her chair and grabbed the cleaver from the roast daring him to continue.

Sivia covered her eyes with her hand. She could tell by his expression that Gerstan's nerves were shot. She thought: next open window he sees, and I'll never see him again.

Father went quiet, but gave her and Gerstan one last glare each, before turning to his food, eating with a frown still on his face.

#

Sivia slipped into the room shutting the door behind her. She did a little spinning dance move that was really a duck and riposte without the sword, and an added not so subtle swivel of hips. She didn't own any fancy lingerie, so she made do with a clean shirt unbuttoned in suggestive places.

Already in bed Gerstan gave her move an appreciative whistle.

Her strut across the room had too much of her customary stalk in it, but it was all about knowing your audience, and he liked it. She rattled the bars of his cages with her fingernails as she passed disturbing his miniature captives. One of them yelled a squeaky profanity at her.

She took her time climbing into bed and straddling his lap, making a show out of it, grinding against him like a cat trying to get comfortable. His hands came to rest on her backside with an audible slap. She made the yelping noise he wanted to hear and endured his massage of her ass. She'd yet to break him of the instinctive male desire to knead her softer spots like they were made of dough. That would take time.

She took his hands and moved them around to the front of her hips where he had a better idea of what to do. Leaning back with the rest of her body to press her lower half into his fingers and get him on the right track.

There was loud banging sound from downstairs. Gerstan's eyes widened and a chill ran down her neck. They were trying to untangle themselves even before the banging ended in a crash.

Sivia snagged her sword from the rack and flew for the door.

"Torches," Gerstan said from the window. "Lots of torches!"

She was already in the hall, sprinting for the stairs, drawing her sword, not caring that she was half naked. There was yelling. Already she could hear combat. Her heart was pounding. She was worried about her parents, angry at having invaders in her house, angry at being interrupted.

There was the clank of armored boots coming up the stairs, and she met a knight coming up. His sword was still sheathed. He reached for it, and she cleaved his head in half spilling its liquid contents into the rim of his gorget. Sivia pushed past him, his body taking too long to fall. She changed direction at the landing and jumped the lower steps.

She found the downstairs a battleground, a battle her parents were losing. Knights packed the rooms almost shoulder to shoulder.

Father was being backed into his study by four men with thick bladed, cleaver like, short swords. He was swinging a fire-poker at their faces, and screeching Goblinac curses.

Mother was in the kitchen. Wearing a night gown, with her hair up in curlers, she was frothing at the mouth and swinging her spiked 'hog killing' club. With every swing, men were sent flying. Her mad, raving rant about 'cooking them all for Sunday supper' had them scared, keeping the ring of men around her too timid to attack and press their advantage.

Sivia charged the knights attacking her father, running the first one through the back, killing him before he could even turn around. But when she tried to withdraw her sword, she found it stuck. So, when the huge sergeant beside him whirled around to face her she had nothing to block with.

She abandoned her sword and jumped back just in time to avoid losing her head.

The knight plowed towards her, ignoring a kick to his knee which hurt her foot more than him.

A gauntleted fist connected with her jaw. It felt like an explosion in her head. Her vision flickered for a moment, and she felt a tooth, or multiple, come loose in her mouth.

She staggered backward and would've fallen if she hadn't

run into a wall that managed to prop her up.

Dazed, Sivia watched the fight end miserably for her parents. A sword finally caught Father, and she heard his bones crunch. On the other side of the fight a man with a spear got himself set behind the shield men and killed her mother like a hunter would a bear. The old woman killed three knights in her death throes.

Sivia would have died too right then, if the man who hit her had struck immediately instead of taking the time to stare at her bare legs. They must have been desperate in the army.

By the time he did attack Gerstan's knife was there to catch it. Gerstan deflected the blow and sunk his knife through the seam of the man's armor at the arm pit, plunging it in to the hilt. The knight fell over mewing like a dying cat.

She wasn't crying, but he must have guessed from her expression because he didn't ask about her parents.

"We need to go," he said.

"Where?"

From one of the cages that adorned his belt, he removed the red fairy. The little woman gripped in his hand screamed and pleaded up till the moment he bit her head off. Gerstan upturned the dead fairy like a shot glass, draining the twitching corpse of its juices; then turning to the group of knights standing between them and the door, he spat it back out. As it left his mouth the liquid burst into a giant fireball that would have made a dragon proud.

In a two second flash twenty some men were torched. Steel armor blackened, their skin bubbled and cracked, falling apart into a gooey ash. The smell of burnt flesh burned her nose, but when it was over there was a clear, smoldering path to the door.

Walking backwards, Gerstan glared at the remaining knights, keeping his mouth shut and his cheeks puffed out, as though he could perform that trick again. When their hands were on the door latch, He pulled the green fairy. Snapping its legs like a wishbone, he threw the dying creature to the floorboards. Where it hit grass appeared, followed by vines and leaves.

They bolted outside, slamming the door shut behind them, and holding it. The house shuddered and creaked as an acre of forest tried to fit inside. There came screams that were shortly muffled. Branches shattered through the windows, and the door bowed out cracking around its hinges.

Then everything was quiet. Sivia was starting to cry now, even as she breathed a sigh of relief. Her parents were dead, her childhood home destroyed.

But she and Gerstan had made it, just a little further.

She turned around just in time to see a wooden pommel break Gerstan's nose. Gerstan wobbled on his feet for a moment, and just when she thought he was about to say something sarcastic he fell to the ground, out cold.

Sivia snarled at the man in white.

He was older than she'd expected. His face was heavy with lines and he was nearly bald. What little hair still clung to his head was white and thinning, almost translucent in color. He wore no armor, no marks, just a blank tabard over ivory robes.

She snatched Gerstan's knife from the ground beside him, tossing it from one hand to other, and back again.

"I'm going to break that toy sword over your head! And then, I'm going to gut you, old man, pull all your guts out, and knit myself a sweater out of them."

He brought his wooden sword down to a low guard with a flourish.

She lunged at him, feinting for the thigh then reversing her grip at the last moment and swinging up, aiming to stick the blade in his chin. She missed. The man in white dodged her blow with a calm fluidity. He was fast for his age.

That pissed her off. Screaming profanities at him, she charged into his guard swinging at whatever was offered: his neck, his chest, arm, neck again. She really wanted to open his wrinkly neck. But, her every attack was dodged or blocked. She'd get close, and yet the man in white never even looked concerned. He was fast for any age.

A sweeping kick to her ankle stumbled her, stopping her charge, and the man in white spun around her in a mono-color flash, ending up behind her. The blunt edge of his wooden sword came crashing down into her back just above her hip.

She wasn't sure if she heard a crack or if the searing pain just overloaded the rest of her senses forcing them to join in. It took her breath away. She let herself fall to the ground, rolling forward and coming back up with a spin to face him again, hoping the movement hid how much that had hurt.

The man in white leapt, bringing his sword over his head and down in a strike meant to break her arm or shoulder. She caught it on the knife bracing her wrist with her other hand. Pushing his weapon aside as hard as she could, she tried to force him out of position to block, and then charged him again wielding the knife with both hands throwing power blows. When he dodged, she'd come in again staying close to him. When they literally collided, she drove her knee up into his ribs. It landed with a satisfying impact and bent him over with a groan.

His chin forward, she threw an uppercut connecting perfectly and standing him back up. His eyes sort of glazed and she expected him to be out. She lashed out for his neck with the knife.

He dodged: leaning back just in time. Her blade missed his throat by the smallest of measurements.

And, now she was off balance. The wooden blade came up into her right wrist with splintering force. Bones broke with a sickening pain and then her whole hand went completely numb and useless. Her fingers let go of the knife. She tried to catch it with her other hand, but it had reflexively gone to clutch the other.

The man in white was already in motion.

He spun his sword around him bringing it back then lunging out in a kind of stab she'd never seen before. His arms barely moved. All the motion was completed by a twist of his legs, the power driven from his hips. The blade of his weapon smashed into her abdomen with an incredible impact, bugging her eyes and momentarily ending all thought.

Sivia fell to her knees.

The man in white brought his ridiculous sword back to a guard position with the same flourish he'd used before. The tip had broken off, and her blood stained the splintered blade. It was a lot of her blood.

A euphoric, warm feeling spread from her stomach out to the rest of her body. The body's way of patronizing you, and sure proof that something was really wrong.

The man in white raised his weapon, twisting slightly about to throw his whole body into cracking her skull open. She just watched him.

He never struck the blow – instead he screamed. The man in white stiffened, sucking in a long breath he held till his face turned red.

It was like watching a cricket stung by a scorpion. His eyes became soggy then turned into black goo that drained from their sockets. He fell to his knees, and then all fours. The black liquid flowed from his every orifice in enough quantity to indicate everything inside of him must likewise be melting. His skin cracked around the joints, blackening like burnt paper at the edges of his ears and fingers, before the husk finally collapsed inward and the man in white became just white clothes slowly sinking into a hideous soup.

It was sight that demanded respect for the cave fairy.

Gerstan stood behind the mess. Blood streaked out from his busted nose, and he was smiling. Black gore still stained his lips.

Sivia tried to get up and found she couldn't. The hand she clutched across the hole in her stomach was soaking in blood, and as a whole her effort to keep her innards in was failing.

"Sorry," She told him, "but I'm not going anywhere."

His face fell. "Does it hurt a lot?" He asked in a gentle tone. She shook her head no.

Gerstan walked to the edge of the trees, took the money pouch from his belt, and threw it as far he could.

"What are you doing?!" Sivia screamed at him, then doubled over in pain from the effort.

He walked back, plopping down beside her in the grass. He put his arm around her shoulders.

"Get off me," She ordered, using her free hand to push his arm off. "Go get our money and get the hell out of here!"

Gerstan lay back in the grass, looking up into the darkness of the trees.

"Cave fairies are poisonous," he said matter-of-factly. "I was going to use her for my arrows. They're not so good for you orally."

She stared at him for a moment in disbelief. "Well that was stupid."

He chuckled.

"He already had me!"

Gerstan shrugged.

Wincing as she did it, Sivia eased herself back so she could lay with her head in his lap. "I was lying," She explained. "I didn't want you to feel bad, but since you went and acted like an idiot, of course this hurt. I have a hole in my stomach.

"I'm sorry."

Reaching up she found his arm and draped it back over her.

"We didn't get real far, did we?" She said.

"No…" He was starting to sound sleepy, "…not too far." He had one of the gold coins in his hand and was rubbing it between his fingers. "You know what?"

"What's that?"

"I'm really glad your mother bit that one guy's nose off."

Sivia smiled. "So am I."

HALF A CENTURY - OLD OR YOUNG?

By Duanne Walton

Nobody's asked me to share any words of wisdom from the past fifty years.

I wouldn't know what to tell them.

Sorry. No profound insights from the edge of middle. More like garbled fragments from the edge of the abyss.

When I was a young man, I didn't know what every young man was supposed to know. Now I'm going to be an old man, and I don't know what every old man's supposed to know!

I should be celebrating this milestone. Instead I'm adulting. This is what being an adult feels like? I'll book the next one-way flight to Neverland, please. Just don't ask me to wear green tights.

Memories swallowed by the white noise in my head. But not the humiliation and abuse of peers, bosses, and authority figures. Messages received and understood, but they're still screaming at me.

Not the glazed pleading stares just as I'm about to have the energy sucked out of me. I know, I should've been honored to have been the light in their darkness. Honored that they looked to me in their need. But need was all they ever had, only giving back frustration and aggravation. I had to distance myself before I ended up pointing a gun at the backs of their heads while telling them about the rabbits. And they hadn't even killed anyone.

Why couldn't these be swallowed, and the good things remain?

Maybe because then I'm more thankful for what I have now.

I have *real* friends that strengthen, not weaken.

I have places where my friends and I gather: my church and my writers' group. They are my sanctuaries and safe places that I always anticipate.

I have creations to make: stories, videos, dances and comics, and declare them good and share them with the world.

And above the storms in the sky and in my mind, beyond all we see, hear smell, touch and taste, is the one that makes it all possible. The Creator and Master, whether acknowledged or denied. He that gives new days, mercies, and opportunities. He that gifts talents and abilities. He that loves us.

Do I have words of wisdom from the last half century?

Not really.

Just fear forward and be thankful.

Always be thankful.

HIGH VENUS OF WILLENDORF

By Annette Gonzalez

a nubian mane
stirs in rhythm with
the wind, whipping
dangerous dancers into
frenzied fray and
caressing the air
in the midnight
plight stream

body: a mere sketch
of a figure crossbred
with the surrounding
circumference

a sandy torso emerges between
absolute chiaroscuro and stone

beauty is transformed, though
lost in the strata of obscured
pebble jewels of ages past

once planted into the
earth, prayed to and
preyed upon, the small
gentle, fertile
emblem emerges
again out of
absolute
chiaroscuro
caressing
the ages
and
blessing
earth
once
more

I SURVIVED AN ENCOUNTER WITH A YETI AND SO CAN YOU

By Diana Estell

In Memory of: Sir. Reel Newton, Deranj Mindstill, Lance Livingston, and Alan Awol (missing). May their lives and discoveries live on.

I will relive my harrowing ordeal with a Yeti, plus list twelve easy survival skills you will need to escape a similar unfortunate attack. All previous and subsequent events are actual and factual.

I have no memory of being rescued. In a tent, on the border of the Himalayas, a Buddhist monk gave me tea and writing supplies. A peaceful presence draped the monk's body, nothing flashy, just a dull age-worn orange robe. His bow brushed away my attempt to thank him for everything. The only other survivor, one of my colleagues, lay in a fetal position shaking and mumbling on a cot.

Five scientists from Expedition Everest, set out from the U.S. in early summer. We arrived in Kathmandu, then set out shortly to our appointed research base. There is a fearful beauty here. Majestic mountains clearly project the size and scope of how small humans are. All of us should have latched onto the fearful part long enough to let humility set in, and thus potentially avoid the Yeti attacks.

In the name of science, I left common sense back in my tent. I wanted to document a rare species of flora, which only bloomed in the dusk. While drawing a quick sketch, I heard a deep crunching noise behind me. Cautiously, I turned my head and jumped a mile out of my skin when a gigantic white shaggy beast burst out between two trees as if they were matchsticks. A deep growl rumbled inside its thick chest. Through parched lips, I tried to scream, but the shallow words ran on the winds of despair. It was all or nothing now. Do or die. I tried everything and nothing all at once. Boy Scouts failed to prepare me for something like this. What a cool badge that would have been: You're Ready for A Yeti.

Not far from me, I saw several other colleagues in a similar predicament. The furious, ferocious, flesh scraping, claw and jaw ripping, spikey wigged out furred Yeti lumbered closer to me. Big globs of saliva dripped from the corners of its snarled lips. Dashing, dodging, and doing this and that, I escaped, but the others… Numb, clammy, and nauseated, I pushed my pencil on. If whoever reads this and heeds my warnings and advice, you will live. If you don't, you won't.

Don't Drop from My Flops. Rise Triumphant

The Yeti are not mythological or legendary, but real. They reside in Forbidden Mountain ranges. In other words, do not enter. Get a map from the Nepal embassy and find out where these mountain ranges are located. Not all Forbidden Mountain ranges are accounted for. Ask the local Sherpas, they have the best up to date knowledge. Don't even think about venturing into, discovering, or wandering around these parts. It is highly unadvisable. You've been warned. Wish I would have been. Out of my original twenty-four options for survival, I condensed it to twelve, as these worked.

1) Prevention is key. Don't go to the area they live in. They are very territorial and guard and protect their territory fiercely.
2) Prevention by distraction: jump up and down.
3) Wildly flail your limbs in every direction.
4) Shout very loudly, as I believe the Yeti to be deaf, or seriously hard of hearing.
5) Do numbers 2 through 4 at the same time.
6) Play dead standing up. They react to movement. Don't lie down and play dead, for you will be.
7) Repeat over and over to yourself. "I love the environment." I think Yetis are mind readers. This is the fearful beauty I wrote about earlier. Respect the environment. Yetis have no tolerance for pillaging their land.
8) Don't litter.

9) Stop, drop, and roll. Yetis like entertainment.
10) Sing. Suggested song choice. "I love the environment." If you can't carry or hold a tune, don't sing. This is a time when faking it 'til you make it will cost you more than your vocal cords.
11) Give them money to donate to their local conservation chapter.
12) Run, run, run.

The monk smiled down at me and gave me something to eat. I stifled a laugh at the English writing on the package in front of me. The Big Yak Attack from Yakkety Yak. *It's no Big Mac, but Yak.*

IN HIS HEAD

By Alfredo (Freddy) Gutierrez

The sound of white noise filled the living room as Dysart came back into consciousness.

He fell asleep on the couch again as he often did on school nights. The room was dark, lit only by the soft glow of the television. Dysart looked around for his phone wondering what the time was but secretly debating if it even mattered.

After a few seconds he pulled the phone from in between the cushions. He pressed the power button and the screen came to life ... barely.

"Nothing out of the ordinary ... no one cares ..." Dysart thought.

But in reality, too much was going on ... two missed calls, five new messages, battery life two percent, and the time was 3:07a.m.

Dysart stood up and wiped off the runaway saliva from his mouth. He fought the tingling sensation on his legs as he weaved his way past sleeping dogs and furniture to his bedroom. Once inside, he plugged his phone into the power outlet and undressed himself. He stared at his reflection in the body length mirror that leaned against the wall. He looked at his messy hair, the bags under his eyes, the lumps of fat that formed his body, and his overall uneven complexion. He shook his head trying to unsee what only his eyes could see.

The next day at school, Dysart walked the hallways with his eyes on the ground wondering why no one liked him ... why no one ever took the time to say hello to him ...

Because he didn't look up, he never saw Ricky, Joe, or Allen waving at him to join them for a friendly chat. He never saw Rachel giving him flirty looks or the group of kids that admired his drawings posted by Mr. Reese moments prior. Because he had his earphones on, he never heard Amber and Ellie talking loudly about him. Talking about how they admired his tall, lean, and slightly muscular physique. How they loved the hazel color of his eyes, his spikey hair or how they adored the way his cheeks created dimples when he smiled.

Smiling was something Dysart rarely did anymore.

In English class he scribbled words on a sheet of paper attempting to write a poem. He crossed them off and rewrote them several times. He never noticed Megan across the classroom staring at him with gentle eyes.

When the bell rang, Dysart crumpled the sheet and tossed it away missing the waste basket.

"It's garbage," he thought.

As the students made their way out the classroom Megan picked up Dysart's waste. She had always had a soft spot for him. Some could even say she was in love with him. She placed the crumpled piece of paper in her pocket and walked to the restroom.

There, inside a stall, Megan unfurled the ball of paper and began to read. Shortly after starting, her lips trembled, her hands shook, and her eyes quickly turned to liquid. She let out a sigh and pressed the paper against her chest.

"It's beautiful," she said as streaks of mascara ran down her face.

That night, as Dysart went through the front door of his home his parents awaited his arrival in the living room.

"Dysart …" his parents called out as one.

"Hey guys," Dysart replied smiling.

"Sweetie, we're leaving in the morning, why haven't you packed your bags?" his mother asked.

"Because I'm not going," Dysart thought.

"Yeah, aren't you excited to hit the beach … and check out the girlies?" his father asked.

Dysart's mind dashed to hide the dark thoughts within the confines of his head before they spilled out without control.

"Be normal! Act normal!" his brain shouted.

"Of course, I am. That's all I can think about. I'm so pumped about this vacation. I just couldn't decide what to bring with me, that's all. I want to impress all the girls. I want to take the island by storm. I want to leave Hawaii a married man," Dysart replied still smiling.

His face was lit up like a child's on Christmas morning. His parents laughed, he laughed, and the dogs barked and wagged their tails. Dysart was as happy as he had always been … on the outside. On the inside the 17-year-old boy screamed. He shouted as loud as he could, crying for help. But no one heard his pleas. No one knew his pain. No one would come to save him.

Later that night when the house was quiet and its inhabitants slept, Dysart gathered the ingredients he needed to make himself feel better. The time to lay his head to rest had arrived. Months prior when Dysart still had the energy to appear happy, he had collected a few things from his friend's homes. He took a bottle of OxyContin from Ricky's house. He took a bottle of Xanax from Joe's house. And he took a bottle of vodka from Allen's house. He hid them in a hole on the wall of his closet hoping he would never have to use them. But the pressures of his make-believe life were far too heavy nowadays.

Without stopping to reconsider, Dysart took a handful of pills from each bottle. He threw them in his mouth and washed them down with the vodka. The burning knot carved its way down reminding him of the reasons why it had come to this. His eyes watered with more than just physical pain. He took his phone to check the time. It was 2 a.m. But he also saw that he had four missed calls and fifteen new messages. As he looked through the call log, he noticed each one of his once best friends had called him along with Megan, the girl he secretly crushed on.

"Why are my friends trying to reach me, why is Megan?" he questioned the phone.

He moved onto the messages and noticed several were from days ago. Again, his friends had tried to get in contact with him. They invited him on trips to the mall, trips to their favorite hangout spots, and trips to their homes. Megan commented on his drawings and praised his creative poetry on social media. She even asked if she could stop by his house one day to see other completed pieces.

As the messages got newer their tone changed. His friends were now concerned for his well-being. They wondered if they should ask someone for help. They wondered why Dysart ignored them.

The top right corner of the screen on his phone read twelve percent battery life along with the time, 2:25 a.m.

"What's going on?" Dysart asked himself out loud.

He couldn't understand why he hadn't seen the messages or missed calls before. He wondered why his social media accounts had been desolate just moments before. He felt the urge to reach out to his friends. He tried to reply to one of the messages, but his fingers refused to move. His vision began to blur, and his breathing became too heavy for normal living.

"Fuck … the pills …" Dysart said remembering the lethal cocktail. The words echoed in his ears.

He looked at the time, it was 2:47 a.m. and the battery life was at four percent.

"I have to call for help …" he thought.

Just then his legs gave in and he fell stiffly to the floor. As the phone slid out of his hand, his finger touched the camera icon bringing the front-facing camera to screen. The phone bounced on the floor and rolled to a stop against the wall. Displayed on the screen Dysart saw the handsome boy that everybody saw. The flaws that he had seen time and time again had existed only in his head. Everything had been inside his head. But it was too late for regret. It was too late for redemption. It was too late for anything.

As his organs failed and his heart stopped, all Dysart could think was how much he wanted to do the only thing he could no longer do: live.

"I don't want to die … I don't want to die … I don't want to … I don't want to … I don't …"

Dysart died at 3:07 a.m. That night he was on everyone's mind.

IT WASN'T ME

By Allison Rios

No! Never! I'm supermom! Although, with my husband scowling at me (with his eyes squinting so tightly I'm worried his head might explode - partly due to a very long day at work and partly because he knows I am not the one who cleans the house) I'm starting to think maybe it is my fault. I'll never admit that out loud and on the record, but it's entirely possible I made a bad parenting decision.

I must not have received the "eyes in the back of my head" that God supposedly hands out to all mothers. Surely if I'd had them, I would have seen Alex reaching for that bottle. Yet five feet away from my turned back, as quiet as a mouse, he grabbed that bottle and shook it all over. That's right; that innocent bottle of fresh-smelling goodness went swirling around his head as he shook like a go-go dancer with a mission. I only caught a quick glimpse of the fascinated wee one with the fresh-scented plume gracefully falling around him before he quickly put the bottle down in slow motion without ever making eye contact. He stared straight ahead as though that would prevent me from seeing him. To a two-year-old, eye contact equals guilt, and he wasn't about to cave. The white cloud enveloping the living room was blatantly obvious, but he became a perfect statue as though I would never notice the white film covering his entire body.

I almost wanted to give him a high five for his commitment to pretending it hadn't happened. Almost.

In that moment, staring at the computer screen and a monstrous load of work while some crazy cartoon echoed loudly in the background, I realized there were two ways to go with this: I could start screaming at him for making such an incredible mess (and believe me - it was a fantastic mess), or I could laugh it off after a very stressful week at work.

I went with laughing. I mean, in the grand scheme of things, it was pretty hysterical. He had magically created a tropical snowstorm in my living room. No one got hurt, and nothing was damaged. I had to stifle a laugh as I thought about the fact that my house smelled a heck of a lot better after "the incident."

I walked towards him and the tears began to form in his sweet little eyes as those tremendously long eyelashes batted the tears away. One tear made it down his cheek by the time I got to him. Well, halfway at least. It stopped mid-track because the powder had thickened it up. Alex was completely white from head to toe. He looked like a ghost with just his big brown eyes peeking out from the layer of powder.

I knelt to his level and smiled, then laughed – and it wasn't a fake laugh. Despite the enormous cleaning task ahead of us (okay, let's be honest – my husband), it truly made my week! It was just about the funniest thing I'd ever seen as I looked around at the hardwood floor, couch, and coffee table that now resembled a cocaine dealer's manufacturing plant.

My husband did not share my sense of humor on this, and I can't blame him. Tired after a long 12-hour shift, still in his uniform and nearing time to go to bed, he did clean up most of the mess.

While I laughed hysterically, almost falling-on-the-ground laughing, the vacuum spread the powder again and blew it back up into the air with every pass he took. While he swore vacuumed, I regained my composure and brought some wet towels to try and pick it up without spreading it.

My son didn't know what to think. Once we had him changed into clean clothes and smelling fresher than he ever had – and probably ever will again – we tucked him into bed. Then, in the hopes of a little relaxation, we went down to watch some television in our newly cleaned room. We both plopped down on the couch and met with a poof of baby powder. At that point, neither one of us could hold back giggles.

The next morning, everything in the area was coated again by a light baby powder mist. And so this scenario went on for two weeks. We had the freshest smelling house, and someone learned two precious lessons.

That person, by the way, was me. I learned that sometimes, you have to find the joy in even the difficult things because otherwise, you could miss a truly remarkable experience that will enhance you as a mother. And the second?

Never, ever, under any circumstances, leave baby powder within reach of a toddler unless you need a laugh.

We all make mistakes, but the key is learning to turn the mistake into a memory.

Like the time I drank the obnoxiously orange slushie. Ah, I remember it like it was yesterday.

I really don't like orange slushies and yet there it sat, glaring at me from the cupholder. It was nearly full, and I really didn't want the too-sugary, weird orange flavored drink that doesn't even taste like a delicious orange. It's like black licorice with a taste that just isn't what I imagined for a treat.

But I was determined to drink it. Maybe not all of it, but most of it. There were two big, brown eyes staring at me from the back seat watching to see if I would. She knows I don't care for orange popsicles and orange freeze pops, so I'm sure she wondered if I would like the slushie.

But I wouldn't.

And yes, I still drank it.

We had just stopped at her favorite ice cream shop in town and she wanted to get something different than her standard order. She was buying.

She ordered an orange slushie and I ordered my fave - a cherry slushie. The same one I've had at that same ice cream shop since I was her age.

She paid and we hopped back in the car, off to the next errand. I glanced in the rearview mirror and saw it - the wrinkled brow and the "ew" face. I asked if she liked it and she said it was fine, and then softly asked for a taste of my cherry – which is also her fave. Her face echoed of regret for her choice of flavors, and she pretended she would be happy with just one sip of mine.

"Can I taste your orange?" I asked, and she handed me her cup. I took a sip and realized it's as awful as I imagined, but I wasn't about to show it.

"How about we trade?" I ask.

"It's okay, mom."

"I really like yours, though. You'd be doing me a favor."

She let a smile slip and tried to hide the excitement of such a serendipitous score, her orange-disliking mom actually liking something orange. "Okay," she said as she happily started in on the cherry ice.

And I fake smiled back as I sipped the orange monstrosity.

Maybe some people would frown on the white lie of pretending to like something we don't. Maybe some would use it as a lesson to teach their kids to not waste money. I wouldn't begrudge anyone thinking along those lines - I've definitely done that.

Yet that day, my daughter was kind enough to treat me to ice cream. In her life, she will be adventurous. She will make many choices. Some she will be happy with, and some she'll look back on and wonder why she didn't make another. For many of those times, her tears will fall, and her heart will break and despite all my love and hugs, I won't be able to take that regret away.

But that night... well, that night I could remedy that regret and salvage her special treat for the price of 15 minutes slurping that gross, orange slushie. Let me tell you, her smile was worth every single sip.

Because that's what moms do. We kiss the boo-boos, we eat cold food after everyone else is done, we help with the math when they're frustrated, we cheer on their wins, we give them the last piece of pie, we hold their hands when they're heartbroken, and we love them fiercely no matter what.

And sometimes, we just drink the orange slushie and bask in the baby powder.

LIKE ALL SUCH STORIES (an excerpt)

By Jessica Harris

Like all such stories, it should begin in the ancient way.

Once upon a time, I found myself stranded in a rainstorm. Without the benefit of lightning, the path before me was dark. Expecting a quick journey, I didn't take a horse, a fact I now regret. My feet sunk deeply into the ruts and mud and I ambled miserably through the torrent to find a dry place.

I was soaked to the bone and was constantly wiping the rain from my face when the warm light of fire appeared before me. My relief bubbled its way out in a giddy laugh that turned into a damp cough. Bundling up against further assault, I made my way hurriedly to a large alehouse called "The Compass Point." It was two crooked stories of wood held together by rusted metal and necessity with a stable off to the side. But for now, it was dry and welcoming and that's all I wanted.

Inside I found much what I was expecting: a fire to warm my outside, strong ale to warm my inside, company for the time, and welcoming hosts.

My hosts were a husband and wife. The Host was a stalwart man whose ruddy complexion bespoke of much time spent in a tankard and was dangerously close to losing himself to it. Even now, his head was thrown back and his man lump moving up and down like a dog's tongue, the honeyed ale dribbling down his mammoth beard and chest.

My hostess was much more courtly, though it was evident by her round build and large flat hands that she was of common stock. She would smile warmly to all her guests (all brought in from the horrendous weather), though her eyes were quick and calculating and I had little doubt that she could keep a drink as well as her husband and keep books to penny precision.

Hell hath no fury, I noted to the observation. While I hate to brag, I'm a quick judge of a man based on the way he held his cup; I find that a man can lie in any and all other areas of his life, no man can lie to his drink.

Sitting to my left was an older man whose long grey beard was a knurled mess of tangles. His kind face was crinkly, speaking of a lifetime in the sun, though his eyes were shaper than a knife. He nursed his drink like an old lover. Both knew their positions well. They both knew how many tankards it would take before he fell completely under her spell. Argument between them there was none as they participated in their common, comfortable promiscuity. He was not yet under her complete captivation.

To my right was a boy hardly twelve years old. He was dirty and unkept.

Pick Pocket I thought the moment I saw him.

While he kept his shoulders and spine still, I could sense his legs bouncing from pent up energy and no small amount of anxiety. He watched everyone carefully, his own drink hardly touched. It was a big brother that, while the first few harmless pranks would be ignored, would quickly turn and beat him down for obstinance. He had this fight before it seemed, based on the way he drank so warily.

Beside Pick Pocket were brothers of soul, not blood. A stronger kinship ne'er can be formed. One was dark in every way, while the other was freckled and still retained an air of boyish charm despite being the elder. These two laughed and whispered amongst themselves and with Host (who sat near them), spilling their drink as an offering to God.

God protect drunks, fools, and children.

These young men were clearly just weaned from their parents' purse strings and had not yet understood the value of the pennies they were spending. No, they instead asked for constant replenishment of their glasses; the more they drank the more they fed to the floor and the less they cared. They each were the careless boys of the drink, the ones whom Ale would be quick to pounce upon when the tab was due. But for now, I would not rob them of their wasteful merriment.

Rounding out this group of misfits was the man sitting a little ways away from the group, somewhere oddly between Hostess and Old Man. He watched the interaction of the people around the table with the nose and lip curl of superiority. He alone did not bear traces of the inclement weather: no spot of water on his tunic or cloak, no moisture in his hair. He must have been there long before the sky broke lose. What a man of his obvious distaste would be doing there other than necessity I couldn't wager a guess.

He was dark like Dark Brother, only his was not a darkness cloaking inhibited joy. His darkness was from the inside out. He was sorrow, pain, and suffering. He sipped his drink slowly, cautiously. He would raise his tankard to his lips and pause, breathing in the aromas of the glass. Then he would drink a little, just enough to wet the tongue and pour past cracked lips. Pull back enough to breathe it in again before lowering it.

It was a servant-master relationship, I realized. The role changed frequently. One day he would be the Master, able to drink to his heart's content and not feel one ill effect of fire in his veins. This was a useful skill to have when engaging with vagabonds and politicians. But the roles could be reversed, and when drink was the master, he would be uncontrollable, flying into vicious rages and bloody conflicts.

Based on the sharpness of his gaze, I guessed tonight he was the master. Sorrow must have sensed my study because he looked at me. His eyes dared me to say something, to do something, but what I was unsure. A sudden loud slamming sound called my attention to the other side of the table. Light Brother was slamming his tankard against the table through his tear-induced laughter. Black Brother had his head in his arms, his shoulder's shaking in happy hysteria.

These poor boys didn't realize how far gone they were.

"Do you have anything to eat?" I asked Hostess. She tore her eyes away from the Brother's antics to look at me.

"I'm sure I can scrounge up something warm for ye," she said kindly. "That'll be a ha'penny."

"Simple enough," I agreed.

"Me too," gruffed the old man beside me. In fact, it wasn't long before everyone at the table was calling for food. All except Pick Pocket.

"And the boy," I said, fishing into my pocket and pulling out a penny. She nodded as she got up, turning and slapping her husband as he had pinched her backside.

"Leave it, you scoundrel!" She said, though there was affection in her words.

"If you think on it, I have a sausage I need something done with!" He said, much to the roaring laughing of the Brothers. She rolled her eyes and disappeared, coming in a few moments later with a stack of wooden bowls and several loaves of bread. She disappeared quickly, returning again heaving a heavy pot of some kind of stew. She set it down with great effort, wiping her brow. She then began to ladle the contents into bowls, breaking off a sizeable piece of bread and handing them around to those who paid her for this work. Pick Pocket stared at the steaming bowl ahead of him, even as I tore the slightly hard bread into pieces and dropped it in. I nodded toward him.

"Go on and eat, son." He nodded and pulled the bowl closer to him. I grabbed his wrist, which had found its way near my purse. "Don't think on it." He met my eyes, waiting for me to loudly protest or announce his sin to the crowded room, earning him a lashing and a kick out the door. "I've purchased you a meal, so show some deference. Guard my things and ensure no one else makes off with them and you'll get a ha'penny in the morrow."

"As you say, sir." Pick Pocket said. I let his wrist go and he recoiled it instantly as if I was wearing hot iron. I chuckled softly into my own bowl. Pick Pocket picked his bowl up and with astonishing speed and no manners he shoveled his food into his maw.

I knew hunger.

"What is news, then?" Host said, starting on his fifth or sixth tankard of the near score he would drink that night.

"I hear the prince is still missing," Gruff said into his bowl more than to us, flecks of root vegetables clearly visible in his nest of hair. He lowered it and looked around. "Been, oh, I don't know, two cycles now? Nobody knows."

"He was kidnapped, I hear." Light Brother said. The glassiness of his eyes might have to do with sharing gossip, but I guessed it had more to do with drink.

"I heard he run—ranned---he left on his own," Dark Brother said. His I *know* was drink.

"Highly doubtable." Sorrows voice startled me. It was higher in pitch than the deep, earthen voice I imagined. Despite its till, it was still one that covered the ground of authority. "The prince would have no reason to leave; especially with the upcoming celebrations."

"He should turn up," Hostess said. "If it was something to worry about, there would have been soldiers knocking down my door, you mark my words," she said, pointing at Sorrow with her spoon. "But they ha'n't. Nah, he's hiding somewhere for who knows why. He'll turn up, I say."

The strange company fell into silence as we finished our meals. Hostess brought out fresh drinks for everyone, taking the eatery away.

"I hear there's an old saying in these parts," I said when the opportunity arose. All eyes shifted to me between curiosity and stupor. "Something akin to 'five to the men, ten to the witch.' What does it mean?"

"Are you new around here, boy?" The old man said. I nodded, but then shook my head.

"I'm not from too far, but I've never been here, and I certainly never heard that expression."

"In these parts," Sorrow began. "It's said that the during the Dark War when witches ran rampant, they were beaten back into oblivion by five; it means a smaller amount of something is better than a bigger amount of the other."

"Nonsense!" Host roared. "There's no such thing as witches!"

"But there could'a been!" Light Brother slurred. "There – I say there could'a been!"

"Here! Here!" His friend agreed, sluggishly holding his cup aloft with no idea what he was agreeing to.

"Drunkin' scoundrels!" Host slapped Light Brother on the back of the head, sending him flying forward. "I say again: there's no such thing as witches!"

"I saw a boy in the streets once," Pick Pocket supplied. We all looked at him and he flushed so red I thought he'd burn on the spot. "He said he'd been cursed, and at night we could hear him screaming like an animal." He shuddered. "It was terrible."

"Sounds more like a sickness than a curse, child." Hostess said warmly, but Pick Pocket shook his head.

"I know what I saw! His eyes...."

"You know, I heard that too." Dark Brother said, uncharacteristically sober and the boy gave him a small smile that could be relief.

"*Bah.*" Hostess said. "It sounds like gutter stories with a minstrel's flair, nothing more." With our stomach's content, we all sat back, enjoying the conversation.

"Does anyone know a tale?" Gruff asked. "All this talk of missing princes and witches puts me in a foul mood for digestion."

"I do!" Light Brother said. He cleared his throat now that everyone was watching him. He stood up like a herald in a market square ready to announce the birth of a prince or marriage of a duke, one hand on his hip the other straight into the air. "*It was a night in yesteryear, surrounded by fog,*" he began his drunken recitation and quickly heard boos and laughs as his friend dragged him down into his seat.

"You don't know half of that tale, you twit," he said with a vicious hiccup. "You probably can't even remember all of the characters!"

"I can too! Let me see, there was Alaric the Brave – everyone knows that one, then there was…." He faulted. "The sword guy. What was his name?"

"Guarin, and you're doing him injustice, don't you think?" Sorrow said. "You're talking about the greatest swordsman who ever lived."

"He was not! There's no way he did all the stuff they said he did."

"Like what?" Pick Pocket asked, eyes alight.

"They say he was able to cut through solid stone with his sword," Light Brother leaned forward conspiratorially. "That no man was able to best him with any kind of blade – be it sword, knife, or dagger."

"Poppycock," Hostess said. "Well, at least cutting through stone. I've never heard of a single story that says he could that."

"So do you think it's true?" Dark Brother asked. "That he was the best?"

"Hard to say, really. It happened so long ago that who knows what he actually could have done. I wouldn't be surprised if he really was the best swordsman in the kingdom; I also wouldn't be surprised if my son could beat him!"

"He couldn't." Gruff said. Everyone looked at him. He shrugged and went back to his drink.

"Anyway, who else was in that tale, boy?" Host asked somewhat jokingly.

"I completely lost track," he said.

"Lost track? We've only mentioned two!" I said. He looked at him, face already ruddy.

"Two what?"

"I take it *you* know the tale?" Hostess asked.

"Well, I –" Everyone jumped at a sudden thunderclap. We turned our attention toward the window. "I'm familiar with it," I said, turning back to the group.

"Do you fancy yourself a storyteller, then?" Host asked.

He waved his cup toward Hostess, who scoffed as she grabbed it and disappeared, returning a few minutes later with a few fresh cups: one for Host, two for the drunk boys, and one for me.

"An amateur, in a way." I said with a slight shrug.

"An amateur storyteller?" Hostess asked. "How is such a thing possible?"

"Well, I've some practice here and there telling stories, but I haven't made a career of it." I said, somewhat embarrassed by the intensity of the gazes on me. "Cycled a bit when I was younger; made a few pennies. Nothing really worth noting."

"But you've done it?" Host said.

"I suppose so, yes."

"I'll tell you what: Give it a go. Tell us a story – no! No! Tell us *his* story," he said, pointing at the drunk boy. "If I enjoy it, I'll not charge you for the room tonight."

"You won't?" Hostess said with a bit of a warning. Host was oblivious.

"Nope." I glanced at Hostess whose nostrils flared, but she said nothing. "Tell it exceptionally well and the meal and drinks are free as well. What do you say?"

"I'm afraid you give me too much credit," I said, looking for an easy way out of offending the hostess. I didn't have the heart to tell him I already paid for the food for me and the boy. It wasn't long before everyone in the inn was calling for me to begin the story. Sighing, I shook my head.

"Well, the version I know is a little different than the one that's conventionally told," I began, but was met with a strange silence.

"Different?" Sorrow said, his tankard clacking against the wood. "How so?"

"I heard the popular version told only once as a lad. It didn't make sense to me because so much was wrong – not creatively interpretation kind of wrong, but flat out distortion of the version I grew up with. I heard it through oral tradition from my grandfather. When I asked him why everyone else told a different tale, he told me it was told to him by his father and so on, coming from the mouth of a guard who was there; he said this is the *true* version of events."

"Is that so?" Host said, sitting back smugly. Dark Brother was snoring, head on the table while Light Brother seemed to realize he'd had a bit too much to drink; the way his eyes focused and unfocused made me realize he was starting to fight against the effect of the alcohol. The slight pink tint to his cheeks said he was losing the battle – at least he would in the morning after he slept off the worst of it. "Well, I think I'd be right in saying that we'd *all* like to hear it now." I nodded to Light Brother.

"Where he began with Prince Alaric the Brave running away from the palace is – I understand – where most begin the story. However, in order to understand the events that led to his running you have to go back farther to the lost part of the story. To another dark night much like this, fifteen years before…."

LIMITS

By Holly Coop

Why let jealousy
Strife
All the other dramas
Of life
Limit you?

Why allow those walls to surround?
They only serve to obscure the view
Where joy can be found
Where freedom is unbound

Why let those brick walls form around you?
Threatening to block what was created to flow
Love
Joy
Energy that shines

The only thing that limits
Is the limitless, of time

LOOK OUT

By Todd Hogan

Tyler sat bolt upright in the stolen gray SUV, looking out for any sign that their job might go bust. His phone timer was set: three minutes. His motor idled, parked around the corner from the First National Bank. Light early morning traffic. Bright sun peaked beneath oncoming, rumbling thunderheads. Sunlight flashing off east-facing windows nearly blinded him.

Fifteen seconds. Nothing out of the ordinary. His Queen CD played "We are the Champions." Tyler had to smile.

Thirty seconds. No sign of Marcos or Beau yet. Marcos had gambling debts that he needed to clear, like, yesterday. Marcos was pushing to do the job like his life depended on it. Beau wanted to buy a new mouth, tooth implants. That can't be that expensive. If Stacy didn't need the twenty-thousand dollars so damn bad, he might never have gotten involved with them. He'd depleted his savings for her, but it wasn't enough.

They originally estimated two minutes minimum, but forty-five seconds now seemed an eternity. At three minutes he would leave without them, as agreed. His sweaty hands, covered with latex gloves, choked the steering wheel.

The car's AC didn't cool the large dark interior for shit. Sweat pooled in his eyes underneath his semi-transparent mask. A hoodie shaded his face and covered his blond hair but added stifling warmth. He forced fingers under his mask to wipe his eyes clear. It didn't work. His eyes gazed through fog.

One minute, fifteen seconds. His breath was trapped by the plastic mask. He feared becoming woozy, passing out, or suffocating while the phone's timer raced toward zero.

A minute and a half. Would he see them when they came? The more he worried, the more rapid his breathing became; the more moisture formed under his plastic mask.

Two minutes. He ripped off the unforgiving mask. He sucked in huge gulps of air, twisting his head to look for anyone who might see him. No one. Nothing. Nada. "You're My Best Friend" rocked.

Knock-knock. Scrape.

He heard the sharp metallic rap on his driver's side rear window. He contorted to look over his shoulder, expecting a uniformed guard, or bulging policeman, or eye-shaded FBI guy. No one. He exhaled the breath he'd held captive.

Two minutes, five seconds. Nearly time to leave.

Krick. Scritch. Knock.

Another noisy clatter at his rear window. Still no one. He wiggled the sideview mirror until he saw someone. A little guy, five or six years old, knocking at the window with a blue conical rocketship. Tyler lowered the rear window.

"Get out of here, dude," he hissed.

The kid frowned. "You got my Spidermans."

#

"Go away, dude. I don't have any toys." The kid wore green shorts sprinkled with orange pineapples, Velcro sandals, a pale yellow tee shirt with pastel blue trim. His green eyes drilled Tyler.

"I left my Spidermans in the back seat." The kid pounded scratches onto the SUV's side panel with his dangerous blue rocketship.

"Stop that! This isn't your mom's car. It's...well, it's somebody else's car. I don't have your Spiderman."

The kid stopped. His green eyes pooled with tears and his lower lip quivered. Tyler searched for some responsible parent to take the kid. No one.

"Where's your ma?"

"Still sleeping. I want my Spidermans!" Louder this time.

Tyler scanned the streets. The kid's decibel level was increasing. He probably had a volume knob that could be set to 11, like Spinal Tap.

Thunder rumbled down the streets. Heavy raindrops painted blotches on the sidewalks. The kid looked into the rain, his eyelashes fluttering the drops away. Tyler pressed the switch that let the rear door glide open.

"Check it out. There's no toys back there."

The kid pulled open each pouch, saw nothing. He dove into the third row to check under those seats.

Tyler's phone squawked. Three minutes! Time to leave. He checked one more time and saw Marcos and Beau sprinting toward him.

"Go, go, go, go!"

Marcos whipped open the front passenger door and pulled himself into the seat. Beau, laughing, ran to the open rear door and jumped, butt-first into the seat, sliding the door closed after him. They shook the rain from their hoodies. They pulled off their masks, gulping air. Marcos's neck tattoo showed--a lone wolf with his left paw raised in protest. He pulled out his .38 revolver.

"<u>Vámanos, vámanos.</u>"

Tyler wrestled the stick shift into gear and the SUV jerked into traffic. "Bohemian Rhapsody" blasted. A maroon Ram truck slammed on its brakes, avoiding collision but sounded its angry horn and flashed its disapproving lights.

"Found one!"

The kid popped up, holding a red-white-and-blue action figure coated with dirt and muck from underneath a seat. He pointed his rocket at Marcos in the front seat. "Is that a tattoo on your NECK?"

"What the...?" Beau jumped off his seat.

Tyler looked back through his rear-view mirror at the kid and his uplifted action figure. "That's Captain America." he said.

"I don't care if he's Wonder Woman, what's he doing in here?" Marcos growled, still holding his .38 revolver. He pulled a brown paper bag from under his hoodie. It looked light.

"He thinks his toys are in this car. I told him no, but he started to make a scene."

"Put him out," Marcos said, pointing with his pistol.

"We agreed no guns," Tyler said.

"Like they were going to give us money because we ask politely? Get real. Now, pull over."

"But, Marcos," Beau mumbled, "the kid's seen our faces."

Marcos frowned at the boy. "Where's your home, kid?"

The boy recited the address mechanically, adding the city, state, and zip code.

"Whoa!" Beau said. "That's like a thousand miles from here! Are you sure that's your address?"

The kid repeated the information, then tried to fix Captain America onto the blue rocketship.

"Well, what are you doing around here?" Beau asked.

"On vacation."

"Stop the car. Just put him out," Marcos ordered.

"In the rain? No!"

"I want to go home."

"We'll get you back, dude. Don't worry."

In the back seat, Beau pull two handfuls of cash from the brown paper bag.

"Are you crazy?" Marcos shouted. "If there was a dye-pack in there, we'd all be wearing yellow paint!"

"About eight-hundred bucks, in toto. Eight hundred! But you got lots more, right, Marcos?"

Marcos pointed the bag away from his face while he dumped the contents. Nothing exploded. The money looked to be about twenty-one-hundred dollars.

"This isn't enough," Beau said. "You said we'd grab thousands. This is nothing, per se!"

"It's less than a thousand a piece, Marcos," Tyler said.

Marcos pointed to Tyler's regular car, waiting in the parking lot of a run-down Greek restaurant. His red Camry looked untouched. The earliness of the morning and the unexpected rain probably helped to protect it. The stolen SUV would not be so lucky.

"Pull in. Switch cars. Leave the kid."

Tyler's own ten-year-old red Camry still ran well and fit four easily. Its trunk held his guitars, pedal board, amp, mikes, and cords to connect them all. Tyler pulled next to it and all, but the kid clambered out. Marcos and Beau jumped into the red sedan. Tyler popped out his CD, mid "Another One Bites the Dust."

Tyler stood between the two vehicles, regarding the scared kid. "Come on, dude."

"My Spidermans!"

"I'll buy you a new Spiderman. Come on."

"Promise?"

Tyler grabbed the boy and shoved him into the Camry next to Beau.

"What are you doing?" Marcos barked. "Kidnapping is a federal rap."

"So's bank robbing. I guess we're committed."

"That brat's face is going to be streaming on every channel, TV, and computer screen. Phones will post his picture. Nobody cares about a two-bit bank job, but you steal a kid, now you're talking mucho trouble."

"I didn't sign up to steal kids, per se," Beau said. "I just wanted to get my new teeth."

"I'll worry about him. You guys figure out how to get the money we still need."

#

Tyler drove to the old-style motel where they had rented a room for the week under false names. The motel, scheduled for demolition in six months' time, didn't ask questions.

They dodged raindrops running from the car to the door of the room. Their rooms, in the back, faced the train yards. The kid stopped before entering, entranced by the stately, plump yard engines nudging cars to form trains. He winced at the loud crunch when a car slammed into the existing line which shivered with the impact.

Tyler pulled him into Marcos's darkened room. Brown and gold shag carpet snagged his sandals as he stumbled in. Two double beds with faded deep green covers took us most of the room. Two poles held three groups of lightbulbs. The newest piece of furniture in the room was a flat-screen TV.

"Ughh! What smells?" The kid wrinkled his nose.

"Probably the water," Tyler said, pointing to a faded warning printed on copy paper near the sink. "Don't drink the water. It's rated B."

Beau parked himself at the round table near the room's one window and dumped out his brown bag. "Eight hundred dollars. Not enough, Marcos. How much you got?"

Marcos tossed him the paper bag with his cash. "Not enough." He sprawled on one bed, his hands behind his head.

"This is less than a grand for each of us. Less when we pay for the room and food. We need a new plan," Beau said.

"Shut up with the kid around," Marcos said to the ceiling. "Get rid of him, Tyler. Or I will."

Tyler stood next to the kid and pointed to Marcos. "You just figure out where we get the money."

"I'm thirsty," the kid said. "I want to go home, but you promised me a new Spiderman."

Marcos sat up, grinning. "Here's an idea. Go get him his toy, Tyler. Go to Walmart. They have shelves of toys there. And..." he leaned forward, "...they have security who take care of lost kids." He caught Tyler's eye to be sure he understood.

"What's your name, kid?" Tyler asked again.

"Rocky."

Beau burst out laughing, covering his mouth with his hand. Even Marcos smirked.

"Your real name, kid." Tyler put his arm on the kid's shoulders protectively.

"Rocky."

"Okay, Rocky," Beau said. "The nice man is going to buy a Spiderman. But you have to promise not to tell anyone about us, okay?"

Rocky nodded his head. Marcos shook his head and fell back on the bed.

"If you guys need money, why not go to the ATM?" Rocky asked. "It's loaded with money."

Marcos chuckled. "There's an idea. Can we use your pin and ATM card, muchacho?"

Beau punched info into his phone. Tyler guided the boy toward the door. He took two hundred from stacks on the table, showing both men what he was taking.

"Damn nice toy," Marcos growled.

"Holy..." Beau exclaimed, reading his phone. "Did you know an ATM holds two hundred thousand bucks?"

"I doubt that," Tyler said. "Even so, we can't get in."

"Hulk could get in. He'd just pull and pull until it exploded." They all looked at Rocky, who was making movements with his arms like he was prying open something. "Grrr-awwlll."

"We don't have anything like that," Tyler said.

"Hey! Yes, we do," Beau said, sitting straighter in his seat. "At the repair shop. We keep it for emergency work. A cutter/spreader. Battery operated, too."

Marcos paced the small room. "That's loco, right? Estupido. It's a kid's idea."

"I can get the spreader, no prob," Beau said. "One good job would be all we need, right? Then we're done. Boom! Marcos, you pay off your markers. Tyler, you buy Stacy whatever she needs. I'll get my beautiful new smile. Veni, vidi, vici."

Tyler opened the door. "I'll be back after..."

"Wait, man. Drop me at the shop. I'll get the cutter/spreader. Okay?"

Tyler waited for Marcos's okay. He shrugged but nodded. "Bring burgers. And remember, kid, you never saw us, or no toy. Got it?"

Rocky's green eyes were huge, but he agreed. He kept his arms close to his side.

"Let's go," Tyler said.

#

The rain had stopped, and the gray clouds were turning cirrus white. Bright blue patches filled spaces between clouds. Beau climbed in the passenger side; Rocky crawled into the back. Tyler glanced back before closing the motel door.

"You're going to be here when we get back, right, Marcos?"

"How far do you think I'll get with so little money, huh? I need a sizable score, Ty."

In his car, Tyler picked up a Rolling Stones CD. Because he felt jumpy and uncontrolled himself, he went with

"Beggars Banquet." The edgy percussion of "Sympathy for the Devil" perfectly matched his nerves.

He dropped Beau at the repair shop. "Should I wait?" Tyler asked.

"No need. My truck's in back. See you at the motel. Ciao!"

Beau leaned in before closing the door. "So, you trust Marcos?"

Tyler didn't answer. He pulled away, letting the motion close the door.

As he drove, his thoughts cascaded. The first job had been a bust. There was no guarantee that this plan would be any better. After all, it was based on a kid's fantasy, right? The more he thought, the more he realized he would not be able to get the money Marcos's way. Maybe he should just get out now. Marcos had gambling debts. Beau wanted a new smile. He was not doing this for personal gain, but for Stacy. Even after the job this morning, he had nothing more to give her.

Then he remembered his music equipment in the trunk. He hadn't been able to sell any of his songs, and the bands he played with were struggling for jobs. That road seemed to be a dead end. Almost as dead as the bank jobs.

He didn't drive directly to Walmart. He pulled up in front of Big Pawn.

"Whoa!" the kid said. "Look at all that stuff. Why is it in cages? Are we getting something here?"

"No, dude. I'm getting rid of something here."

Tyler opened his trunk and hoisted his amp and two guitars. He opened one guitar case and ran his fingers along the fretboard, enjoying the silky feel of steel strings against his callused fingertips. "Stay here," he told the kid.

"No way."

Inside, Rocky's eyes glazed over when he looked at the musical instruments lined against the wall. His smile grew bigger the longer he stared.

Tyler quickly came to a deal with the pawnbroker. He had no leverage. He needed the money.

"Just don't sell any of these too quickly. I'll be back with the cash." Tyler hoped he would be back. The owner nodded with a half-smile on his face.

Back in the car, Tyler dialed Stacy.

"Yeah?" she answered.

"I've got to see you, all right?"

"No. Not today."

"I've got more money. It'll help."

She waited a while before responding. "Okay. For a minute."

Tyler drove to her small house in town where the trees had been growing for fifty years. The houses were tiny, but Stacy refused to move. It was a little after noon when she answered the door, her blond hair unkempt, a cigarette in hand.

"Yeah?" she said, not looking at Tyler.

"How are you feeling?"

"Like shit. I don't need any company."

"Stacy, I've got some money. It should help." Tyler dug in his pocket and took out all the money the pawnbroker had given him for his stuff.

"You think I want your charity? I can't pay you back...in money, anyways." She sniffed before taking another drag.

"I just want you better, okay? Here. Take this. I'll get more."

Stacy always looked wasted. She wore an old tee shirt with a band logo too faded to read, cut-off jean shorts, and glasses.

"I guess you could come in," she said.

"No, I have to go. You look beautiful." Tyler leaned forward to kiss her. She turned her head so he could plant it on her cheek.

"Morning breath," she coughed.

"I'll come back later. Take care. Rest up. Okay?"

She nodded as she closed the door.

"Are we going to Walmart, NOW?" the kid asked, his arms crossed.

"Of course. Do you want McDonalds before we get there?"

"Hot cakes is okay. But then we go to the store, okay?"

The least I can do is feed the kid, Tyler thought. He pulled through the drive-up, ordered hotcakes and juice for the kid, and a large coffee with cream for himself. The kid wolfed down the food. "NOW can we go to the store?"

Tyler was still laughing as he tossed the garbage into a container outside of Walmart.

"Stay close, little dude. One thing we're getting, that's it."

"How about a Hot Wheels car, too? They cost almost nothing."

"One thing. I'm not money tree. Find a Spiderman or Black Panther or Superman, I don't care."

The toys were on the left side of the store, the opposite side from the groceries. Tyler found the aisles that he thought the kid would like and got him interested in the action figures. But the kid had other ideas.

"Look at these Legos! A fire engine with a dog! The whole station. And a space shuttle! I think it's a good deal, right?"

There was a wall of Lego kits taking up the entire aisle. It was just what he needed to distract the kid.

"Take your time, little dude. Check them all out. I'm going to get some Cheetos and sunflower seeds. I'll be right back, okay?"

The kid didn't even look at Tyler as he left.

Tyler walked through the electronics department, hoping to lose any surveillance that might have picked him up in the kid's aisle. The flat screen TVs flickered brilliant colors as he passed. Then he stopped. One image stayed -- the kid. His kid. Rocky. It really was his name.

"...heinous crime...missing since early this morning. Surveillance cameras...the boy entering a gray van with two other men..." A few shots of his mother, his father, and two older brothers. "His father's company...reward of $50,000 for information... Anyone with information should call..."

Fifty thousand dollars! That's more than if they robbed ten banks. He had to tell Marcos.

Tyler rushed back to the toy aisle. The kid wasn't with the Legos. He wasn't with the action figures.

"Rocky!"

No answer. Tyler grabbed the large Lego set, a Mars explorer and space shuttle. He checked more aisles, his panic growing. If he never told Marcos, what was the harm? Then again, fifty thousand dollars!

Then he saw him, eyeing the Hot Wheels display. "Just one?"

"Okay. Take one. You have your Spiderman?"

"And a Lego?"

"How's this Lego? A space shuttle! Pretty cool, right. Grab a car."

"Which one? Which do you like?"

"Here's a Tesla. Let's go."

"My dad has one like this, but it's shiny black."

Tyler paid and hustled the kid to his red sedan. They left the parking lot and hurried, without speeding, to the motel. Beau's white pickup was parked outside. He knocked rapidly and Beau answered the door.

Tyler pulled the kid and his packages into the room.

"What the...?" Marcos said, his eyes narrowing on the kid. "You still have a kid? And no burgers? "

"This kid is our money burger," Tyler said. "Turn on the news."

#

Beau found the local news channel. "But what about lunch?" he asked.

"Forget the damn burgers. Keep watching."

When the piece about Rocky aired, both Beau and Marcos stood and approached the TV. Pictures of the kid, but none with his pineapple shorts or yellow tee. The real kid opened his bags and took out the Spiderman and the Hot Wheels Tesla. He left the Lego set for later.

"I don't believe it," Marcos said.

"Fifty big ones! Whoo-ee! I'm talking top of the line implants, per se."

Tyler nodded, watching Marcos react. Marcos squinted and pursed his lips.

"So, I brought the little dude back here so we can decide how to collect the reward."

"Two problems," Marcos said. "First, explaining how we got the kid. We picked him up at the bank? I don't think so."

"They said no questions asked. We don't have to explain," Beau offered.

"They just say that. Second, we need that money now. Not in a week or two, but like tonight." Marcos held up his phone. There was text from an unknown number reading, "Time's up. Tonight. West train yard warehouse."

Beau read it out loud, then said, "It's not a threat, per se. But it doesn't sound good, I admit."

"I need the cash. Tonight. Got it? And not penny-ante. Benjamins or lots of twenties."

"Just explain that you'll have the money, a big score, but in a day or two."

"Don't you think I've told them that already? Get your head straight, Beau. No. We can delay figuring out how to return the kid and collect the reward, but only for a while. But tonight, we hit that ATM. We have to bust that sucker wide. You read me?"

"Okay, okay, Marcos. I didn't understand the situation. I do now. You need the money now. Lighten up."

"It's not your neck on the line, Beau."

"It wasn't me that made all the bad bets, either."

Tyler stood between the two, trying to bring down the temperature of the discussion. "You two go tonight. Go bust open the ATM. I'll stay here with little dude."

Marcos's eyes narrowed. He half-grinned and shook his head. "No way. You're coming with me. The last time we left you alone, we ended up with that kid. I send you to Walmart to get rid of him, you bring back the kids and bags of toys. I leave you alone again, we're likely to find you and a tribe of brats in here. No way. Beau, you stay; Tyler, with me."

"I don't know how to work that machine."

"And I don't want to stay with a kid."

"Beau, shut up. Tyler, you've got until dark to learn how to work it. Beau, help him." Marcos spread out on the bed, his hands behind his head. "Let me figure out how to collect that reward."

#

The kid sat cross-legged away from the men playing with the cutter/spreader. Tyler kept his eye on the boy, who seemed engrossed in his play. After three hours of experimentation and practice, Tyler had it down. Beau stood up and patted the machine.

"There. Now you know as much as I do. I still think I should go, Marcos. Let Tyler stay here."

Marcos scowled. "No. If you want to go somewhere, go get us some burgers already. Guitar Man let us down on that score, too. Tyler, give him some your left-over cash."

Tyler fished in his pocket and gave all of the remaining stash to Beau without counting it.

Beau was gone for about two hours in his white pick-up. When he returned, he had sacks of burgers from Hamburger Heaven and two six-packs of a local craft beer. "The beer took longer," he said.

"The burgers better be hot," Marcos said, "or you're going back for more, and paying for them with your share. Got it?"

"They're hot, I promise. I went to Double H last." He tossed a hamburger to Marcos, and two to Tyler. "That one's plain, for the kid.

"No thank you," Rocky said.

"You aren't hungry?" Beau asked.

"I like chicken nuggets."

"Try a burger. It's plain. Put anything you like on it. The condiments are in the bag here."

"I thought I said no tomatoes," Marcos said, holding the burger at arm's length. "Didn't I say no tomatoes?"

"Sorry, Marcos. You want the kid's? He's not going to eat it. Maybe he'll eat the tomatoes, quid pro quo."

Marcos gingerly plucked the tomato slices from his burger and threw them at Beau.

"Hey, watch it." Beau ducked, then tossed the men each a bottle of the craft beer.

"What is this 'IPA'? Where's the Bud?"

"Some friends opened a mini-brewery. They make this stuff. Taste it. Very citrusy. The alcohol content is like seven-point-five." Beau took a long swallow, finishing with a satisfied "Aaahh." He opened a second bottle. "Remind me to tell you about that place, Tyler."

"Why? They hire bands?" Tyler asked.

"I don't know about that. Just remind me."

"Who needs 'citrusy' beer?" Marcos said after a sip. "It's not bad though. Throw me another."

They ate for a while. Tyler asked, "Any thoughts on giving the kid back?"

Marcos scoffed. "No easy way, Jose. Focus on this job tonight, and then see what we need to do."

Tyler saw the kid listening. "Look, Marcos. I'm gonna take the kid and go get the little dude some nuggets and some pop. He's got to be starving."

"The kid stays here. You want to be spotted? Ruin everything? You're not thinking! Beau!"

Beau quit lining up four bottles on the nightstand and looked up.

"Go get the kid some chicken nuggets and fries and a coke and an apple pie. Then get back here."

Beau uncurled from his side of the bed, tossed his wrappers into a garbage can, stretched, and went into the bathroom.

"Come here, little dude," Tyler said, bringing him to the round table. He put the left-over money on the bed with Marcos. Then he opened the bag with the Legos. "Do you know how to make Legos?"

The kid shrugged. "Follow the book?" He pointed to Beau in the bathroom. "He should shut the door."

"Yeah, shut the door, Beau! Now, go get those nuggets and hurry your ass back." Marcos opened another bottle. "Perdón, Rocky."

Tyler pulled out three full color booklets that showed how to complete the Lego spaceship and Mars rover. He gave the kid the book-marked number one and put the other two aside.

Before leaving, Beau leaned close to Tyler. "Hey, it's not my business, but I saw that Stacy at the mini-brewery."

Tyler froze briefly, then kept sorting the Legos into piles by color. "Yeah? So, what was she doing there?"

"What do you think she was doing there? I just thought you should know. Et tu, Brute. Aaaagh." He mimed being stabbed in the back.

"Get going, Beau!" Marcos shouted. "And be back before dark."

Beau scooted out of the room and slammed the door. The engine on the white pickup growled and barked loudly. Tyler looked around the room for answers. He'd always thought of others first. Today, he wasn't sure how wise his policy was. He could have collected the reward with a single phone call. Let Marcos and Beau explain how they got the kid.

"Now, what?" the kid asked.

"We take it a step at a time, okay? Just follow the pictures."

The boy matched the first few images with actual Lego pieces put together. After each completed page, his smile increased. Tyler checked his phone. No calls from anyone. His power was running low. He could call Stacy later, when he could talk alone. She really shouldn't be drinking while on her medicine. She should be resting, getting better. Or maybe he would just go see her.

"How's that look?" The boy held up the vehicle meant to be a Mars rover for Tyler's approval. With a little imagination, it looked very real.

"Just needs some wheels."

"Could you help with those? And the stickers?"

Tyler put his phone away but couldn't focus.

"You take it easy, Tyler. I'll help the little guy." Marcos finished the rover with the kid. They had just started book number two when Beau returned with food for the kid. Tyler made room on the table for Rocky to eat. Then he leaned back in his chair. He fought his urge to dial Stacy.

After the kid finished with an impressive burp, Marcos helped him build the space shuttle. Beau napped while Friends reruns played on the TV. Tyler's fingers itched, and he wished he could pull his last guitar out of the trunk and start to wail. Playing helped him to think.

It took about three hours, but the kid finished the Lego set. Even Beau had helped, finding the small pieces that fell of the table and into the twisty shag rug. "I'm not looking down there," Rocky said. "It smells awful."

The kid fell asleep about nine-thirty. At eleven-thirty, Marcos went to the bathroom, shaved, combed his wavy dark hair, and tucked his .38 into the waistband of his jeans.

"Leave the gun here, Marcos."

"Protection, man," Marcos offered.

"From a metal box? It stays here, or you and Beau can go without me."

"Chillax." He took the revolver and placed it on the table before Beau. "You watch this, Beau." Then Tyler caught him darting his eyes at the kid. Beau saw it, too, and smiled, looking at the sleeping boy. Tyler felt 'chillaxed' by their behavior. Overall, he trusted Beau, though, and figured no harm would come to the kid.

Marcus carried the heavy device in one hand, pretending to open the air conditioner beneath the window. He laughed and indicated with a head jerk that Tyler should follow.

"Focus on this job. It would solve a lot of our problems, right?"

As they left, Beau called out, "Carpe noctem! Get it? Carpe NOCTEM?"

"Watch the damn kid," Tyler answered.

#

They stole a black Fiat two-door to use. It fit the cutter/spreader easily and both Marcos and Tyler. They left the red Camry at a steak house that had good business this Saturday night. Tyler drove to the ATM Marcos selected. They parked in a grocery store parking lot where they could surveil the Bank and the ATM. It was a well-manicured bank, with attention to the landscaping. It was cut back, but not so much that the ATM was exposed to every passerby. The security cameras were a different matter.

They watched for an hour. One police car drove by without stopping. Four customers used the ATM. Tyler guessed that an ATM that was so little used probably didn't need two-hundred-thousand dollars inside. But he said nothing to Marcos.

After an addition fifteen minutes and two additional customers, Marcos flipped up his hoodie and grabbed his mask. He poked Tyler in the side. "Let's go."

Marcos carried the duffel bag with the machine to the ATM and set it down for Tyler to operate. Tyler looked at the ATM. Where to apply pressure? They should have researched the machines. Where was the cash stashed? High, low, or in several places throughout?

"Go, go, go, go," Marcos said, keeping an eye out for any cars passing.

The ATM was designed for use by drivers. It had a high slot to swipe an ATM card. The video screen was flush with the wall and provided the buttons to push to give the ATM commands. There were additional slots for dispensing money and depositing checks.

"I don't see how this can work, Marcos."

"Just do it. Open it. Cut it or spread it or blow it up, I don't care, but do something!"

Tyler put the heavy metal blades into the cash dispensing tray and pressed the button. The slot distorted for about ten seconds, then burst. Tyler looked in the aperture. No money there.

He put the blades deeper into the widened slot and pushed again. The metal casing tore quicker. He pulled the metal panels wider with his hands until he saw stacks of cash. He couldn't believe it.

"Marcos. Com' 'ere." Tyler pulled out stacks of twenties, dumping them into the same duffel bag they used to carry the cutter/spreader. Marcos dove in with two hands, pulling handfuls of twenties out one after another.

"This is too easy," Tyler said. "I don't like it."

"This is great. Keep pulling out cash until it's gone."

Suddenly, a shrill, pulsating whine assaulted their ears. A bright white light flashed repeatedly, illuminating the entire driver's bay. Tyler grabbed the duffel bag with the cutter/spreader and ran to the black FIAT. Marcos pulled all the money he could reach out, stuffing it under his hoodie. Then he charged to the FIAT.

He was laughing maniacally as he closed the door. Tyler's tires spit loose gravel as he left the parking lot.

"Slow down, my man. Oh my god! Look at this!" Marcos held twenties between his fingers and let it rain onto his lap.

"Too easy, man. It doesn't happen this way."

Marcos's grin split his face. "How do you know how it's supposed to happen? Are you some expert at cracking these ATMs? I didn't think so." Marcos's head swiveled around, checking for pursuit cars, witnesses, other thieves, and other banks.

"There's one," he said.

"What?"

"Another ATM. Go, go. We've got this. Drive up there."

"This is enough, Marcos. Let's go back."

"It's never enough, man. How much is the medicine that Stacy wants, huh? You're gonna need twenty ATMs to satisfy her. She gonna tap you dry."

"Shut up, Marcos."

"Turn in there. Now!"

Tyler pulled into another parking lot across from a bank. He hunkered down to wait while they scoped out the new target.

"What are you doing, man?" Marcos stuffed the cash in the duffel bag to one side, making room for their expected score. "Let's go, go, go!"

"We haven't watched the place."

"We aren't going to. Just get it there and take the cash. Bim-boom-bam and gone. Let's went."

Marcos carried the machine again, but this time held on to it while he tried to slip it into the deposit slot. Tyler kept quiet.

Marcos pressed the buttons to activate the hydraulic gears and distorted the slot after about twelve seconds. Then the machine burst. But unlike the first machine, the piercing whistle and strobing white light started immediately. Both men ran to the black two-door, and Tyler drove them away.

"Okay. So maybe we were lucky that first time. One time lucky, one time not so lucky. I say we try one more time."

"Maybe that first machine was defective, who knows? It shouldn't be so easy. Using the jaws of life was the kid's idea. A kid's idea! It shouldn't work. Let's go back."

"You did something different when you opened the box. You try again. If we're going make any scores, it will have to be tonight, because once the banks see how we get in, they will fix up something to prevent us. Probably by tomorrow morning. So, it's tonight or never."

Tyler didn't say anything, but drove around until Marcos spotted another ATM. It looked more like the first one. Tyler used the same technique as before and they collected like they did the first time. Again, when Marcos stuck his hands deep into the ruptured frame, he triggered the alarm and the strobing lights.

"One more," Marcos ordered.

"No. We got what we need. I'm through. If you and Beau want to find others, go ahead. I'm out."

They switched back to Tyler's red sedan, Marcos still ordering Tyler to stop at one more ATM. Tyler wouldn't answer.

Marcos muttered as he slumped in his seat. Tyler paid him no attention but drove to the motel. The white truck was parked in the same spot. The highway roared on one side of the motel, and the train yard still rumbled with the last few cars getting shoved into line.

Marcos retrieved the duffel bag and the hydraulic cutter/spreader. Tyler noticed the motel door was ajar. He cautioned Marcos to be quiet while he edged closer to the door. He smelled the familiar odor of rotten eggs from the bad water, plus something else -- cordite or sulfur. He touched the door open with his foot. Inside was gloomy dark. The acrid stench of dried blood slapped his nostrils.

"Rocky! Rocky!" Tyler shouted.

"Beau? Beau?" Marcus asked.

No answer. Marcos peaked his head around the door jamb and found the light switch. He flicked it on.

Beau was sprawled over a chair next to the table, arms outstretched, his legs widespread, his head hanging over the chair back. In the center of his chest bloomed the brownish red of the gunshot that had killed him.

Marcos's revolver lay on the table in front of him, holding down a note.

"Rocky? Rocky? Little dude?"

No answer. Tyler searched the small room, but it was empty except for Rocky's toys. Marcos grabbed them and threw the shuttle and the rover into the blue Lego box and carried it close to his chest.

Tyler caught a glimpse of the note left under the revolver when Marcos picked it up.

"The money tonight. We have your kid."

#

Marcos examined the revolver, opened its chamber. "One shot gone." That gave Tyler some hope that the kid was still okay. They clambered into the red Camry. Tyler waited before starting it up.

Marcos stared straight ahead. The money was in the duffel bag behind them.

"Do you know where to meet this guy?" Tyler asked.

"Them. There will be more than one guy there." Marcos's breathing was rapid. He set his jaw and pressed his lips together.

"Where do we go? Some warehouse?"

Marcos shut his eyes and did not reply.

" You can't run away from them forever, can you? How much do you owe, anyway?"

"I've got the markers covered with what's in the duffel. And, yeah, I think I can outrun them."

"You're kidding yourself. One of us has to go to them."

"Don't be stupid. They shot Beau. They'll kill you, too. You've got more than enough money to buy Stacy's love. I've got enough to make a new start somewhere."

The mention of Stacy made Tyler take out his phone. Its power showed six per cent, perhaps enough for one last call if he was lucky. "Tell me where to go, Marcos."

"Start it up. Drive me there. Then you should go."

Tyler cranked the engine. He considered putting in a CD, perhaps the last one he would ever hear. He couldn't choose one, so left the player off.

"Turn left."

Marcos directed him under the superhighway. They circumnavigated the wide train yard. On the west side of the yard were a couple of blocks of rectangular buildings about three stories high, wide and flat, with few windows highly placed. They resembled giant Legos built by railroad barons. These warehouses were designed to store goods and materials delivered in bulk by train. Now many of the structures were gutted. Past a chain link fence, lines of empty flatbed trucks narrowed the approach to a funnel. The gate of the fence hung open.

Tyler parked near a door with a single light above it. Marcos checked his revolver again and opened the door. Outside, he tucked it into his waist band. He pulled the duffel bag from the rear seat. Tyler exited the driver's door.

"It's okay, Ty. You stay here."

"Don't take all the money. Just take what you need, Marcos. How much is it?"

Marcos paused, thinking, then emptied the bag of about half of their score into the back of the Camry. He zipped it shut and hefted it. It still looked heavy.

"There's your half. Now just get out of here."

"Jesus!" Tyler said, looking at the cash in the back seat.

Marcos chuckled. "I'll go first. Give me your phone." He set the timer for two minutes. "There. Gives you time to call Stacy. Tell her you have a story to tell her when you see her, and money. Then you can go or come in to pick up the pieces."

Marcos half-smiled an <u>adios</u>, then marched to the door with the duffel bag. He stepped inside.

Tyler waited, heard nothing. His phone life was down to five per cent. He opened his car door and dialed the phone while sneaking to the warehouse door.

#

The metal door opened outward. Inside he saw an empty, dusty concrete floor about the size of a football field. At the far end, two flashlights turned toward him, obscuring his view. He stepped forward.

He kept going until he was about twenty yards away. His phone skreighed--two minutes!

"Stop there! Keep your hands in sight. You should turn around. This ain't your business."

Tyler vaguely made out two men in suits, Marcos with his hands raised, and the kid on a chair. The way the kid moved he was probably tied up.

The men in the suits shuffled, speaking quietly between themselves.

"You aren't getting this money. The tattoo guy owes us. So, just leave." Tyler's eyes had adjusted to the dark. He saw that one of the suits had Marcos's .38.

"I don't want the money. Just the kid."

"You have one chance to leave, buddy. That's more than tattoo guy here. Take it."

"I want the kid."

The suits laughed darkly and raised the revolver.

"FREEZE!" Brilliant lights flooded the warehouse, blinding Tyler and the others. "FBI!"

The suit didn't drop the .38 quickly enough. He was shot dead with one bullet. The other suit pushed Rocky over and hid behind Marcos. He didn't stop there, though, running toward an opening at the far end of the warehouse. An FBI agent stepped in that doorway and barely had time to fire before the suit nearly collided with him. The man went down without a sound.

They focused attention on Tyler and Marcos. "On your knees! Hands up!"

Tyler yelled, "Wait! I'm the one who called you. We didn't know when you'd show up and we didn't want the kid hurt."

"Who's the Mex with the tattoo?"

116

"My bag man."

Marcos grimaced.

"They killed our friend, too. His body is at his motel. When we saw that we knew Rocky was in trouble."

"Gun's been fired," one of the agent's said, holding the .38 carefully so as not to destroy evidence, "and not here."

Rocky went with the agents eagerly. He didn't mention his toys. Tyler and Marcos were taken into custody and transported to a secure facility. Stately, plump agents spent the rest of the night interviewing Tyler and Marcos, nudging them toward a crime, but they refused to be shunted into line. Tyler worried that Marcos would contradict something he might say, but it didn't happen. Marcos and Tyler were released at dawn together. The sunlight flashed off east-facing windows, brilliantly illuminating the government buildings.

"Did they ask you about the money in the car?" Marcos asked.

"I showed them my pawn ticket. I had nothing else. Did they ask you?"

"I admitted I gamble."

"The kid saved our asses. He told them that he had never seen either of us before."

"And he never saw those toys either. Big sacrifice for a little kid."

Tyler harrumphed. "The kid probably has tons of toys. Look at his father. Dripping with money."

Marcos saw Rocky's toys in the back seat of Tyler's car. "You dumping those?"

"Yeah."

"Do you mind? I think I'd like to keep them. Unless you and Stacy want them for your first born."

"That's not happening. First, I un-hock my equipment. Then, I'm out of here."

Marcos smiled. "About time you thought of yourself first, my man."

"What about you, Marcos?"

"I still owe money. Why don't we go on the run together."?

"Sorry, dude. It's every man for himself."

"That's a good philosophy, man. <u>Buena suerte, amigo</u>."

Tyler raised his fist in solidarity as Marcos walked away. In the Camry, he blasted Lynyrd Skynyrd's "Free Bird."

MOUSETRAPS

By Colleen H. Robbins

I saw a mouse today, boldly staring at me as it sat in the middle of my kitchen floor. They're in the walls, too. I can hear them every night, and on cloudy days. Once upon a time, Bert would have taken care of it, but Bert is long gone.

"Stop being so timid, dammit. Take charge and *do* something."

Tears leaked out even before the rest of his words sunk in. Bert was leaving me.

\#

He was right, of course. Thanks to a pack of childhood bullies, I still cringed at any sign of aggression. Unfortunately, that doesn't help against mice.

Calling the exterminator company would be just like calling Bert for help. I could do this. Mousetraps, I needed mousetraps.

SNAP! Clatter, clatter, clatter. SNAP! Clatter, clatter, clatter. Running mice caught their tails and back legs and ran off dragging the traps.

I got up at dawn to a clatter of moving traps. One or two mice blundered into a second trap, ending their misery. A second trap. I moved around the room, dropping a second trap on as many of the hobbled mice as I could catch up with. A few needed a third trap before they stopped moving.

Emptying each trap was the worst part. I took off the first trap or two, then had to scrape the last trap against the side of the trash bag to dislodge the dead mouse.

I slipped into sleep to the sounds of Snap, clatter, and chewing inside the walls.

\#

It has been several days, during which I have mastered my aim at dropping second traps. I am making headway against the mice.

The mice are getting smarter. This morning, I found more missing traps. The mice pushed them into a circle around my bed, facing me. Somehow, they reset the traps.

#

I have not left my bed in three days, now. Hunger is a gnawing pain, and my water jug is empty. I hear the mice chewing every night inside the walls. I used my night shirt to set off mousetraps and make a path to the bathroom and then to the kitchen. I should have thought of this earlier.

I found the refrigerator door propped open and the shelves inside empty of all but some shredded packaging and two dishes full of what looked like black crumbs. Mouse droppings. Yuck.

Worse, the outer doors are surrounded by mousetraps. I cannot leave.

#

The chewing last night was furious, and I hear the slide clatter of traps moving about interspersed with cracking noises and the occasional squeak overhead. In the morning I will leave, I *will*. The sun is barely rising. More cracking overhead.

#

I barely survived. I am so glad I was writing when it happened, or I could not describe my difficulties. The mice are smarter than I thought. A ceiling beam crashed through and landed on me in bed. My bed collapsed on the floor. The beam is across my back, pinning me, but at least I feel no pain in my legs. I fear I may have soiled myself, however, based on the smell.

I hate that the bedding is on the floor. I shall have to wash everything once I get loose.

I can hear the slide and clatter of mousetraps as the mice move them closer and closer to me, ready to add second and even third traps until I stop moving at all.

NEW PRIORITIES

By Kenneth Lee McGee

Editor's note: The following is the prologue to the sixteenth book in The Emmy Series

South Hampshire officer Eric Sanders replied to the dispatch. "En route. Less than a minute out." He hit the lights and siren.

"Fire and rescue are on their way," the dispatcher said. "It doesn't look good according to a witness."

"Call for backup," Eric said as he turned onto Marlboro and mashed the accelerator to the floor.

"Will do."

Eric arrived on the scene and positioned his squad car behind the Civic. He jumped out and looked at the Chevy Suburban which had come to a stop fifty feet away as he approached the Honda. He peered into the car and saw the victim. Just then a man opened the driver's door of the large SUV and stumbled into the street.

"Stay right where you are!" Eric shouted. He heard squad cars and could see a firetruck and ambulance approaching. He looked into the Civic again and, even though he knew the victim could not hear him, whispered, "Hang on. Help will be here soon."

The firetruck and ambulance arrived, and the paramedics rushed over to the Civic. As the first on the scene Officer Sanders issued directions to the other patrolmen. Very quickly the traffic was blocked and the driver of the Suburban, who didn't appear to have suffered any injuries, was placed in the back of one of the squad cars.

"He's a DUI," one of the officers told Eric. "He's oblivious to what happened."

Ten minutes later the paramedics loaded the victim from the Civic onto a gurney and into the ambulance. They immediately left for St. Bart's.

Officer Sanders took a deep breath and looked at the

plates on the totaled car. "FAF1996. That plate looks familiar." He called it in and waited for a response. "Thanks, dispatch. I'll take it from here." He put a hand to his face and then rubbed his jaw. He walked back toward his car and retrieved his cell phone. *I can't do this over the network.* He took a deep breath and dialed a number.

"Hello, son. I thought you were working today," Police Chief Warren Sanders said. "Ray, could you check those steaks?" he shouted at his friend Ray Randich, the SoHam fire chief.

"I am on duty, and I'm at the scene of an accident," Eric replied.

Knowing his son would not call under most circumstances, Chief Sanders said, "Give me the details."

Officer Sanders did and then said, "You know them from the old neighborhood, right?"

"Yes, and I should handle the notification myself."

"That's why I called from my phone. I didn't want the media to catch it on the network."

"Smart thinking." Chief Sanders waved to his friend.

Ray Randich walked over carrying a set of tongs and saw the look on his friend's face. "This can't be good."

Sanders ended the call with his son and looked at Ray. "There's been an accident involving someone we both know, and I need to inform the family."

"I'll drive you since my car is blocking yours," Randich said.

"Thanks. Wayne, would you take care of the steaks, please?" Warren asked his brother. "We have to leave."

"Will do," Wayne replied without asking why.

"Let's go," Randich said. He led the way around the house to his official vehicle. They got in and he backed out of the driveway. "Where are we going?" he asked flipping on the lights.

"Bristol Ridge," Sanders answered. "The Colwell estate."

Ray looked at his friend and swore under his breath.

"Not him." Sanders shook his head. "It's Emmy. His wife." He used his cell phone to call dispatch and arranged for a squad car to meet them at Bristol Ridge.

Thirteen minutes later they arrived at the exclusive development. The security guard saw them approaching and raised the gate. Chief Randich roared past.

"It's the first driveway on the left. I hope the gate is open."

Fortunately, the gate was open and Randich killed the lights as he drove up the winding, hilly asphalt drive. He parked near the front of the house, and the two men got out. They walked to the front porch, paused for a second and then slowly climbed the five steps.

"I doubt they ever use the front door," Sanders said. He took a deep breath and pressed the doorbell two times.

"What was that?" Kenny asked from the kitchen.

"Daddy! That was the front doorbell," Isabella said as she grabbed an apple from the island and raced away.

"Who would be ringing the front doorbell?" Kenny asked.

Rory, who had just entered the kitchen, turned and waved as he walked down the hall. "I'll get it. It's probably Emmy trying to be funny." He laughed as he walked up to the double-door and opened it. The site of two men startled him for a split-second. "You're not..." He stared at the man on the right. "Oh, crap!" Rory muttered recognizing Warren Sanders.

Chief Sanders stared back for a moment, and then said, "Porter, right? Rory Porter from Raynor Park?"

"Yes, yes," Rory stammered. "Come in." Rory backed up and held the door open.

The men entered and waited just inside the door.

"We need to talk to Kenny," Sanders said without elaborating, but his serious expression spoke volumes.

"He's in the kitchen," Rory said. "I'll let him know you're here."

Rory turned and hurried back to the hallway dividing the house. Just as he turned the corner, he bumped into Kenny.

"Who is it, Rory?" Kenny asked.

"It's Warren Sanders and another man," Rory said quickly and then gulped.

Kenny walked around the corner and up to the entryway where Warren Sanders was staring at the floor while Ray Randich gazed at the high ceiling.

Kenny froze for a second before asking, "Chief Sanders, how can I help you?"

Sanders put an arm around Kenny's shoulders, squeezed and whispered, "I'm afraid I have bad news about Emmy."

Kenny clenched his jaw and nodded.

Rory and Rochelle stood in the hallway watching the scene unfold.

"Maybe you should watch the kids," Rory said. "I might need to take Kenny somewhere."

"There's been an accident, and she's on her way to St. Bart's. We're here to take you there," Sanders said.

Rory looked at Rochelle. "I'm going with him."

Rochelle nodded and said, "I will take care of the kids. Call me when you know anything."

"Do I need a coat or my wallet?" Kenny asked.

"No need," Chief Sanders said as Chief Randich walked outside. "We have his SUV and there is a squad car waiting."

"Should I say anything to the kids?" Rochelle asked.

Rory waved a hand and said, "Maybe you shouldn't until we know more, but you should find Father James' number and call him."

"What about her sister?" Rochelle asked.

"Shoot! I forgot about Diane. Could you call her, too?"

"I'll do that," Rochelle said. She kissed him.

Rory saw Kenny's cell phone and grabbed it.

The men hurried to the SUV. Sanders opened the rear door for Kenny. Rory jumped in on the other side. Randich turned the vehicle around and raced down the driveway. A waiting squad car escorted them out of the development.

NOT PETE

By Colleen H. Robbins

It started at the Star City Library. Ariel bent to pull a book from the bottom shelf. Two and three-year-old children streamed past on their way to story-time, their parents trailing behind. Ariel stood and felt a tug at the leg of her jeans.

"Look at me. Look at me." A three-year-old girl with messy brown curls looked up at her, red stains on her chin and hands.

Wonderful, thought Ariel. *I hope the juice stains will wash out. I like these jeans.*

The girl pulled on her jeans again. "Look at me. I am not Pete."

"Well, Miss Not Pete, you need to find your Mommy and get cleaned up for story-time." Ariel walked away, taking her book to an open area with tables. One table held a half-finished puzzle. Ariel sat at the next table, taking notes as she read. A puzzle piece flew by, landing on her table.

The little girl was systematically demolishing the puzzle, throwing the loose pieces everywhere. "Look at me!" the girl screamed. "Look at me!" She had wiped her hands off across her pinafore, ruining the dress. As soon as Ariel looked at her, the girl ran off and pulled at the end of a shelf. The shelf fell apart, books sliding down the now-diagonal shelves and plopping on the floor.

"Okay, that's it." Ariel took the child by the hand and marched her up to the front desk. "This child is completely unsupervised and leaving a trail of destruction. You need to call her mother to the desk right now."

The desk clerk bent over, her name tag dangling. "I'm Lara, honey. What's your name?"

The girl looked up, eyes welling with tears. "I am not Pete."

"I can see that. Do you know your Mommy's name?"

The girl reached up and touched Lara's face. "Look at me. I am not Pete."

Ariel bent over. "Where's your Mommy? Is she here?"

The little girl slowly shook her head, tears welling again.

Lara picked up her phone. A moment later her voice came from the overhead speakers. "We have a lost little girl. Will her parent please come immediately to the front desk?"

Ariel waited for a few minutes. "Should we call the police or something? I feel bad for her."

"Yes, let me call the police. They'll bring Social Services in." The clerk dialed the phone.

"This is Lara at the Star City Library. We have a small child who has no parent with her. She may have been abandoned. Can you send someone?"

A minute and a half later, Ariel saw blue lights flickering as a police car turned into the parking lot and pulled up at the door.

The officer dashed inside. "You called for police?"

"That was quick." Ariel was impressed.

The girl tugged at the officer's pants. "Look at me! Look at me!"

"What is it, sweetie?"

"I am not Pete. You are not Pete."

"I know. I am Ryan." He looked back up. "Excuse me a moment, ladies." He took a few steps away and spoke into his radio. "This is Officer Ryan, responding to that 10-187 call. Repeat the location, please?"

"Star City Library, the back field near the pathway. The witness is waiting." Ryan dashed out the door without a word.

The little girl shrieked. "Look at me!" and followed him out.

Ariel took off after the child. Sirens approached. A battered gray car slowly backed out of a space at the field end of the parking lot.

The little girl stopped and pointed at the gray car. "Mommy car! Mommy car! I am not Pete!" She ran to Ariel and clutched her leg again.

Officer Ryan came closer, taping off the field.

"The girl's mother is leaving! The gray car!" Ariel pointed and Ryan spoke into his radio. A moment later police cars streamed into the parking lot, blocking in the gray car.

The child slipped her hand from Ariel's and ran toward the car, then slowed before she reached it.

Ryan came closer after sending other officers into the field. A young man got out of the gray car and stood talking with police.

"Look at me! Look at me!" The child shrieked, then grabbed Ryan's pant leg. "Mommy car! I am not Pete! Mommy car!"

The officers by the gray car stepped back as the young man opened the car door.

"Wait," Ryan called out. "Who is he?"

"Peter Silverman. He borrowed his friend Cassie's car."

"Look at me! I am not Pete!"

"Take him to the station. Cassie's the name of our vic, and there's a car seat in the back."

Another officer approached from the field. "We found a picture of the child. Social Services has been called. We'll take it from here."

Ariel waved goodbye to the girl and returned to the library. Later, after showing her ID and telling an officer what she knew about the little girl, she went home.

The next morning, Ariel pulled her newspaper out of the bag and nearly dropped it.

SERIAL KILLER APPREHENDED IN STAR CITY
Evan Shamussen, wanted for multiple murders across several states, was arrested at the site of his latest attack. The responding officer held him for fingerprinting after detecting a false ID, according to an anonymous source. The victim's small child, recovered unharmed, has been turned over to Social Services while relatives are contacted.

[Note: This story takes on a darker tone when read for a second time.]

NOTES ON A WALK...

By S. Houk

Animals seen on today's walk (by their tracks): humans, scampering mouse, hopping shrew, dog, coyote, deer, rabbit, mouse nibbling & hopping, the footprints of the sun itself having sunk seed & leaf into the face of the snow, the scratch of a sheaf of grass obliterated by my own footprints, the chirp of a bird, the faraway song of an airplane flying my brother home.

I find a lost cemetery and realize it was only lost to me. I find a sledding hill that appears to only want one thing: me and my sled to visit tomorrow. The only question: will I or will I not fall into the creek.

What I didn't find are the telltale signs of the tips of the wings of a bird of prey sometimes accompanied in the snow by bits of rabbit fluff. No such dinner wasn't evident.

(On the question of how to tell the tracks of coyotes and dogs apart: dogs screw around stopping and starting. Coyotes know where they are going and lope. Basically, coyotes have a destination; dogs do not.)

On a clear day, if you look at the snow at just the right angle, you can see every color sending up sparks. Emeralds. Sapphires. Rubies. You start to not trust your eyes. Surely the world cannot be this beautiful. They threaten to leap up and catch the field on fire - a conflagration of jewels.

ONE MAN'S TRASH

By James Pressler

Three-thousand square feet, every inch packed to the roof with more odds and ends than the mind could conceive. Never had any place looked at once so full and so useless. As Tom looked through the pole barn doors and saw contents stacked from its cement floor to the arched rafters, he realized just how crowded one building could be.

Dave smiled and patted Tom on the shoulder. "See? That's my problem. Grandpa saved just about everything he came across, keeping it for that one day he'd need it. Well, he's gone, and I'm stuck with his house and everything he ever kept." Dave couldn't even face the pole barn. "There's not a realtor around who wants to sell a house with a whole barn full of crap. There's no way to put a good spin on that. What're they gonna say? 'For sale: Four-bedroom farmhouse, five acres, complete with pole barn and forty years of junk.' No sir, nobody's touching this until most everything's cleared out. That's why I called you."

Tom couldn't take his eyes off the wall of random items before him, a monolith of the mundane. Stacked boxes and milk crates soared over ten feet high, filled with too many odds and ends to count, as if every noun in the English language had representation. Crates, suitcases and duffel bags mingled with buckets of metal fittings and pipes, all resting on table tools, saw horses and more. The back end of a Mercury Cougar peeked out from a stack of wooden crates and steamer trunks framing the car, all held in place with a webbing of industrial extension cords.

"Can't you get one of those salvage companies to come here and just tear it all out?" Tom shook his head in amazement. "This'd be a gold mine for them."

"Yeah, but they charge by weight. I'd basically have to sell the house just to cover the bill. And those places want someone on site to manage the move. I can't take time off from work every day, drive all the way out here, then stand around and tell them to throw everything out."

"Ah," Tom nodded. "So you figured since I just lost my job, I could be the one standing around telling them what to do."

Dave cringed. "Well, not exactly. Don't get me wrong – I know you have some time now. But then I figured you're pretty good at just diving into a project. So I thought…"

"You want me to unload all this?!"

"Well…"

Tom looked back at the barn, its contents now appearing twice as high. "And do what with it?"

"Well…" Dave shifted his weight about, sheepishly tipping his head. "Take the useless stuff to the back of the lot and burn it. I doubt there are any heirlooms in there, so just sell the rest for scrap." He straightened his posture a little. "You can keep anything you make off it."

The mere thought of the task made Tom's back ache, but Dave made a good point. Tom only had an unemployment check and his severance to live on for the whole summer, so selling scrap metal would bring in a little extra money. That Mercury alone would get three-hundred dollars at a junkyard, maybe more if it ran. Some of the table tools could go on eBay. There was some value in this trash, even if that value was by the pound. Tom couldn't believe what he now considered.

"So, what's the timeline? How long do I have to drag everything out and burn it out back or whatever? And that is, if I take the job."

"A couple months?"

Tom let out the deepest sigh possible. "I'll start clearing this out Monday, assuming I get the salvage on everything. And I do mean everything." As Dave smiled and reached out a hand in agreement, Tom put in an addendum. "Well, to be fair, if I find a big box of gold doubloons or pirate treasure, I'll cut you in on some of it."

Dave winked. "If you tear through all this crap and at the end of it all find some gold coins, you've earned every one of them."

Tom shook on the deal then turned back to the pole barn, its contents looming larger than ever.

It better be a damn big pile of gold coins.

Tom opened the pole barn doors early on Monday morning, ready to face his project for the summer. He still felt sore from yesterday, when he volunteered to help his friend Michael on one of his many bizarre projects. Last month they tried to fix the brakes on Michael's 1974 Datsun, but needed a grocery list of parts that hadn't been available for a decade. Yesterday they tried to shore up the deck on the back of Michael's house, but without the proper jacks and supports, the project went nowhere. And now Tom went from one hopeless project to another – three-thousand square feet of junk, stacked to the rafters. This was living.

A project such as this could overwhelm a person when viewed as a whole. Nobody could ever clear out a wall of junk by hand, and Tom knew it. Instead, he believed in targeting one area, one object, and dedicating the time to one manageable task. Tom started with the obvious – clear out the space around the Mercury Cougar. One mission – dig out the car for the junkyard to claim. One project to be completed by a series of small, manageable tasks. Just move one crate, one trunk, one item at a time. One step to begin the journey of a thousand miles, or in this case, the journey of three-thousand square feet.

One wooden crate resting atop a steamer trunk stood out as the first item to move, and Tom grabbed it. He wrapped his arms around it, pulled it close, straightened his back, bent his legs and lifted it off the steamer trunk. The bottom of the crate broke, wood fragmenting everywhere as the crate's heavy contents poured out, landing flush on Tom's work boot. Tom threw the broken crate aside and hopped in pain, filling the morning with every obscenity he knew. He turned to kick the contents in frustration, but the sight of what lay scattered on the floor stopped his foot in mid-swing.

The crate had dumped out several steel joist supports and a set of hydraulic jacks, along with several heavy-duty mounting bolts. Yesterday, his friend Michael spent hours cursing the heavens for not having the very things that now sat before Tom. These things could be put to use immediately, or at least once Michael wanted to shore up the deck again. Was this just good fortune, or a sign that plenty of things here might have a use to someone, somewhere – anywhere, for that matter. Was it coincidence that he found the very things he needed yesterday? This meant too much to just be good fortune. It was a sign. Tom gathered the jacks, stands and bolts together and hobbled back to his car.

After dropping off the goods at Michael's, Tom spent the rest of the day online, scouring the local chat boards and social media pages, writing down the needs and requests of everyone in the township. He was amazed to see how so many people sought so many simple things – Mason jars, garden hoses, hand tools, power cords; needs abounded. Tom wrote down three pages of those little things someone needed but everyone else took for granted.

Nobody cares about the little things until they don't have them, then those things are impossible to find and everyone has to scramble to find a replacement. Tom thought of the junk drawer in his apartment – the junk drawer everyone has in their place – and wondered how many people at any moment needed one specific thing that sat in Tom's junk drawer. Now, he had a three-thousand square foot junk drawer, and he would see to it that nothing went to waste.

The next day he arrived at the pole barn at first light and started pulling out trunks and boxes with renewed energy. Everything he opened revealed something on the checklist. Someone needed Mason jars – six-dozen jars still in the shrink-wrap boxes, packed underneath a table saw (and someone else needed the table saw). Garden hose? One-hundred feet still on a wheeled holder. Hand tools came by the box, some in their original cases. A place for everything, and everything in its place. He emailed each of the people he found on social media, providing directions to the pole barn to pick up that one needed thing. And when someone came by, offering a handful of crumpled singles for a simple garden hose or a box of extension cords, Tom just said, "Take it. You're the one who needs it, not me."

The more Tom searched the internet, the more need he found. And as the list grew, the pole barn revealed more treasures. A gross of two-by-fours went to a man adding a nursery to his house. A woman took a full set of furniture, including end tables and a buffet, to replace what she lost in a fire. Five pallets of shingles went to a family desperate to repair their roof. And the man who took the shingles knew someone who wanted to fix up a car for his son, someone who used to work on Mercury Cougars. With a fresh battery, he drove it off the lot with a honk of the horn and a joy Tom had never seen before. Tom reveled in these moments to where he no longer cared for payment. He no longer wanted it.

Tom rounded up the last piles of clutter with a push broom uncovered by the workbench. Over the past two months, the three-thousand square feet of clutter had been reduced to a scattering of boxes on the shelves and by the workbench. The only evidence of the mountains of stuff in the pole barn were greasy outlines where tons upon tons of every item imaginable once filled the space. Now, the broom bristles scraping against the cement echoed throughout the empty pole barn, the last remnants being swept away.

At the beginning of this project, Tom expected to have trash bonfires every weekend. Only one modest pile of scrap sat in the back acreage, mostly disposable water bottles Tom brought every day. All the activity was in front of the barn, where two months of traffic matted down the grass. Tom still couldn't grasp the entirety of what happened – every single thing went to someone. Every need had been fulfilled. Tom had been willing to write it off to coincidence, until last week when he uncovered a box of spare parts to a 1974 Datsun – just like Michael's. At that point, coincidence fell away. There had to be purpose behind this, or magic, or some intervention. He was a practical man, but right now all those concrete beliefs no longer made sense. The most likely explanation was that he had become Santa Claus. Highly unlikely, but still the most likely of many unbelievable options. Whether or not that was true no longer mattered. He definitely felt like Santa.

He had never seen so many smiles on peoples' faces, so much joy in receiving the little things. But beyond that, there was something he couldn't explain. Some people had received whatever they needed, then asked if they could look around at what else was in the pole barn. Tom let them go in and scavenge whatever they could find, but nobody ever came out with anything extra, they never found anything other than the one thing they needed. Could any of that be explained? Did it need to be explained? It happened, and to Tom, that was all that counted.

As Tom swept the last of the debris out of the barn, he saw Dave approaching along the driveway, grinning ear to ear. Tom's weekly reports always pleased Dave, but this time his friend's smile expressed utter amazement.

"I had to see it for myself, Tom," he said, eyes gazing across the empty space. "A part of me thought you would've thrown in the towel after a week in all honesty, and I wouldn't have blamed you. I even though about burning it down just to get it out of the way. But gosh damn, you cleaned the hell out of this place."

"Well, I had a little help." Most people in the township helped by dragging something from the barn. They helped the most.

"So, did you make any money off the scrap?"

"I did okay." A few people pushed some money into Tom's hand out of a sense of obligation or pride, but Tom never asked for a cent. Most everyone accepted everything as the gift it was intended to be, and some expressed their appreciation in ways other than cash. The woman who picked up the Mason jars gave him some homemade applesauce. Other people left little thank-you notes and cards. Tom had netted forty-five dollars in cash and a lifetime of hugs and handshakes. Even though he lived on an unemployment check and severance, he valued the happiness the most. If only happiness could pay his bills.

Dave eyed the barn again. "Well, I got an offer on the place already. Someone knew this was going on the market and dropped a bid right away. Maybe they saw you clearing it out and just assumed."

"Maybe." Tom didn't shy away from mentioning to everyone who came by that the property would be for sale soon. Maybe someone remembered. It didn't matter.

"Anything else I need to know about the barn? Find that pirate's treasure?"

Tom shrugged. "No doubloons. Well, still a shelf or two to clear, but I think that ship has sailed." There was no treasure chest, but there was so much more. Someone's roof had been in here, someone else's nursery. The furniture for someone's new home. A car for someone's son. The tools to fix a deck, to give someone a workshop. Boxes of old National Geographic issues now filled a happy collector's library. And Michael's 1974 Datsun now ran just fine. To Tom it was nothing. Maybe Dave didn't value it as anything, but to the right person it meant everything. Tom ran some simple calculations in his head a few weeks earlier and realized he could've made over forty-thousand dollars if he sold all the goods to all the right people. But the happiness was worth so much more.

If only happiness could pay the bills.

"Well, lock up when you're done," Dave said, adding, "not that there's anything left to steal. I'm going to meet with the realtor. We'll be by here later. But seriously, thanks again, man. Really, thanks for everything." After a bear-hug of gratitude, Dave went back to his car and drove off. Tom watched another happy person leave.

Tom leaned on his broom and thought about all that had happened. So many people had that one crucial need fulfilled at this very point, all thanks to a pole barn full of junk. Everyone walked away with a smile, and now after the last few boxes, Tom would walk away too. Back to his apartment, his job hunt, his bills. It was fun being Santa for all this time, but nobody ever asks how Santa paid the bills that followed. Sometimes there is wonder and amazement, but sometimes hidden treasures just stay hidden.

He walked into the pole barn, but his eyes caught a box under the work bench that he hadn't seen before. He thought he would remember such a thing. How could he have missed it? It was as if it appeared out of nowhere.

Could it be possible?

Tom grabbed a crowbar and pried open the box. His expectations had not prepared him for the shimmering luster of the shining yellow metal before him.

He had never seen so many coins in his life. And this box of treasure was just what he needed.

OUR GIFT

By Tom Hernandez

Dearest Riley,

Hello My Sweet Girl. I hope you're having a good day. Based on your constant smiles and giggles, it's a pretty safe bet that you are. You're one of the happiest babies ever. Which is only fair, because you've brought so much happiness to everyone around you in your 11 months.

Truly, you have been a gift to all of us, maybe especially to me.

Speaking of gifts, I believe whenever you get a gift, you should give one back. As I said in my first letter to you, my words are my gift. So, here are two words:

Social Justice.

A very dear friend of mine says that most of my writing centers on "social justice". She's right I suppose, inasmuch as I write a lot about caring about, and for, people who look and talk and act and think and believe differently than me. Who have lived (or are living) a life not my own. Who have not enjoyed the same blessings and benefits.

Clearly these are very big ideas for an 11-month-old to chew on (although you're chewing on everything these days, so maybe not...)

Yet that's exactly my point.

Broadly defined, "social justice" addresses fair relations between individuals and society through the lenses of wealth, educational opportunity and social privilege.

Heard that way, it's easy to understand why so many people hear and see and think about Social Justice -- capital "S", capital "J" – as something too big for them to do anything about.

Yet, as is always the case, the solution to a "big" problem is to chop it down to size. We can – we must – cut all mountains down to manageable molehills.

The challenge of social justice, like nearly every other human-created challenge, is best addressed human to human.

One of these days, you will hear about a man named Jesus. Your parents will decide what you learn about him. As your Papa, I will only say this much:

For two millennia humanity has dissected and debated every microscopic aspect of what Jesus said, what his words meant, and what they could still mean. This immensely complex question has fueled more war, bloodshed and heartache than every other conflict in human history.

Which is ironic and frustrating, because, for me, Jesus' message boiled down to one amazingly, bluntly, almost ridiculously simple point:

Love God and love one another.

How (or even whether) you define "God" isn't nearly as important as that you understand that there's a bit of something special in all of us.

Every human being living every kind of life is a person and has earned your respect (at the very least), kindness, sympathy and empathy by the simple fact of their existence.

Every human being experiences the same longing for comfort, craves the same need for love, searches for the same validation by association.

We all share the same spark of life. Call it God, call it whatever. The point is, we are all the same, same, same. Regardless of skin color or language or wealth or birthplace. God, in His/Her/Its perfection does not create walls. Only jealous, greedy, arrogant Man does that.

In that light, social justice is easy.

Yes! Help fight to ensure Guatemalan coffee farmers fairly profit from their work.

But also support your local employee association because (surprise, surprise) the billions in profits being made by many American companies never seem to "trickle down" to the little guys doing the work.

Yes! Donate whatever you can to feed those starving in foreign countries.

But also give a few boxes of food to your local food pantry to help your neighbors who just lost their jobs or, more likely, are working three jobs to get by.

Yes! Protest for First Amendment protections for everyone.

But also subscribe to your local newspaper to make sure even the smallest voices always have a platform.

Yes! Visit prisons and read to inmates.

But also support your local library so that maybe, just maybe there might be a few less prisoners needing you to read to them.

Yes! Fight for free health insurance for all.

But also donate a few toys to the children's ward at your local hospital or volunteer a couple of hours and give the overworked nurses a much-needed break.

Yes! Help build schools for girls in Third World countries.

But also buy every candy bar or bag of popcorn or tub of cookie dough or magazine subscription you can to support the overworked, underpaid and unappreciated teachers helping our own children to learn and grow.

Yes! Donate to international charities helping the poor, emotionally sad and mentally ill.

But also give to the local homeless shelter, where all three sleep every night, if there are enough beds.

Yes! Pray for God to protect and drape His/Her/Its goodness over everyone around the world.

But also love and help those who need your kind heart here and now. Always remember that we improve Tomorrow by making today's big problems a little smaller.

My dear Riley, social justice is not a burden too big. It is not an option. It is an obligation and opportunity to show and create grace for a world desperately needing it.

That's our gift to give. Yours, mine, everyone's. One helping hand, one open heart, one loving smile at a time.

PASTORAL PLUS

By Colleen H. Robbins

Ranch and Farm co-exist
For the first time in history

The last humans are gone

Their Hatfield / McCoy style feud
Forever at peace

Horses
Run free
Saddles gone
Leaping fences
Still protected
By the heirs
Forever

Centaurs wear ten-gallon hats
Shirtless as they drive cattle

Minotaurs plow the fields

Satyrs play their reed pipes
Guiding sheep and goats home

PROMISE ME

By Vanessa J.C. Stephens

"Of course," she said, "I've come this far."

"You know you don't have to do this. No one will think less of you." Silvia, her best friend, said.

"I'm not worried about that; it's just that... I made a promise."

The girls sat on the cold wrought iron bench looking out over the bridge and down to the dancing sea. Their backs leaned against the cement partition separating the walkway from the two-lane highway. The breeze was light but just heavy enough to keep a loose hair obnoxiously entering Kate's mouth. With a delicate finger she moved the red strand behind her ear.

"Come on Kate, this is not something that should be done lightly. This is a big deal." Silvia said, adjusting her position more upright. Her face reddening at the daftness of her friend.

"You act as if I didn't think about this, I did. I thought long and hard." Kate gazed wide-eyed into the dimming horizon; her sight blurred with tears.

"I know that he would want me to do this," Kate added, wiping away the drops under her eye.

A rumble came from behind the girls' heads by an approaching airplane circling steadily, gearing to land, filled with passengers either happy to be home or happy to have left from where they came. Both girls ran a smoothing hand through their wind-blown hair, still worried about looks even with the low volume of pedestrians on the bridge. Once the roar died down, the girls took hands.

"I'm just worried about you Kate. You've never been this reckless."

"Maybe that's why he made me promise to do this. He always wanted me to liven up." She smiled with remembrance.

"He once offered me a dollar to eat a hot pepper. Ha! He always wanted me to try new things, even if they seemed stupid."

"So did you?" Silvia asked.

"Did I what?"

"Eat the pepper?"

Kate's face dropped. "No, I didn't but I wish I had... Funny thing, it wasn't until years later that I tried a hot pepper on my own and you know what? I love them. All those years wasted and bland because I didn't listen to him."

"Yeah, but this is much different than eating a pepper. Way dumber."

"Yeah, but I have to try."

At that the friends sat in comfortable silence. The passing cars lulled the girls into a mesmerizing trance while the sky turned in a kaleidoscope of colors ranging from blue to orange before their wistful eyes.

Sighing Kate stood and faced her friend.

"Well, I guess this is it." Kate held out her arms as Silvia stood to accept her friend's embrace.

"I don't think I can stay." Silvia said.

Kate nodded sympathetically towards her friend.

"I understand. Do me a favor?"

"Anything."

"Call my mother, tell her I'm sorry. That I needed to do this."

Silvia nodded and assured her friend that she would follow her wishes.

The two girls embraced a second time and then parted ways. Kate watched as Silvia reached into her pocket for her phone and made her way along the bridge towards her parked car. Kate inhaled deeply; the salty air burned her nostrils. She stifled a cough as she climbed upon the cement outer wall of the bridge. The sky a blazing red. Her hair fluttered recklessly in the whirling breeze. A car horn blared startling her. This wasn't the way she wanted to go. It was supposed to be a spiritual moment, not drowned out by the unsolicited honking of car horns.

However, now it was too late. She stood here ready to jump. Her arms extended like a bird--she breathed...

Faintly, she heard a voice ask, "Ready?"

She closed her eyes and whispered, "Ok dad, here we go."

She gasped and with a push of her legs she leapt off the edge.

Her stomach dropped at a speed far greater than the rest of her body. Her breath stalled with the pressure against her face as the wind built up a cold dense wall. Finally she didn't care about her hair or her clothes or the fact that she missed her father. All she had was the wind, the sky, and herself. Her eyes watered and she smiled. Then the bungee tightened and jerked her upwards. Her body limp with released stress, she laughed the whole way back up to the bridge.

RECIPE TO SAVE A MARRIAGE

By S. Houk

Leave your favorite stuff at home.
Get on an airplane with a suitcase.
Don't return until you have:
forgotten what they smell like,
forgotten what they look like,
forgotten that their eyes
contain all the universes
you will ever tumble into -
dark and bottomless
with a laugh at the bottom.
Repeat until you aren't pissed off anymore.
Repeat until you can't find
the universe anymore.
Repeat until they forget
to be pissed off anymore.
Throw away your suitcase.
Return to your favorite stuff.

SNAPSHOT OF GOD

R. Michael Markley

Where should I start? Let's see… no world peace, crime on the rise, and global warming. Then there's inflation that sometimes makes stretching the paycheck from week to week a challenge. Depending on whom you choose to believe, we are either in the best of times or our world, as we know it, is spiraling out of control. There are many things that make us worry.

Do you ever worry? My wife worries all the time. She often asks me, "Don't you ever worry?"

"I try not to," is my usual response. This really doesn't bring much comfort. It sometimes makes her worry for the both of us. At least that's what she tells me. I completely understand that in today's world there is much to be uncertain about; but in scripture we are told to "be still and know that I am God," Psalm 46:10. That is my solace. Those words never rang clearer as they did one morning on my way to work.

Ever see a full moon as it's setting in the western sky? It's an awesome sight. That morning I got another reminder of how certain and how great our God is. How He is in control of everything. Even when we may think the world is out of control, He gave me a beautiful sight to look at on my drive to work. With the picture I was given on this morning, the ride could have lasted an hour and I wouldn't have cared!

You see, I get up very early. My wife thinks I'm crazy but wishes she was a morning person like I am. There are some very gratifying joys I receive from being up so early. A moon set is one of them. When the moon is in its fullest stage and it starts showing itself in the eastern sky, it's enormous. Its glow illuminates the clouds as it travels upward seeming to light up the entire night sky. This particular morning as it was setting in the western horizon, it was also gigantic in size, a beautiful reminder that God is the creator of the universe.

I wanted to go home and shake my wife out of her dreams, sharing the moment with her. I would have pointed to the picture I felt God personally painted for me that morning telling her, "This is why I don't worry." It was one of those Kodak moments. With God there are always Kodak moments. Whether it's watching a hummingbird pollinate or a blue sky filled with white clouds that look soft enough you could jump and play in them all day, you see God in it all. Whenever we look at a photographer's work or a painter's canvas and see the vibrant colors, we look past the picture trying to look inside to see the soul of the artist through their work.

God gives us snapshots of Himself every day so that we can see who He is.

This particular morning my breath was taken away when I saw the moon just sitting there.

I said to myself, "Thank you for the reminder of the great God you are." It was like He was putting His thumbprint on the end of another night or to mark the start of another day opening his world while showing Himself to His creation. As I traveled west it was hanging right in the middle of the road as if God was holding it right in His hands just for me to see. Every once in a while, God gives us something to knock the cobwebs out of our daily lives showing us who He is. We should be grateful.

You can look at the stars at night knowing God placed each one exactly where He wanted. It's reassuring that they're in the same place the next night. Not swirling around all out of control. It's amazing how the sun comes up in the same sky every morning and sets in the same place every evening. The vast expanse of the Grand Canyon or the height of a giant Redwood are just two more signatures of God. We enjoy a gentle rain as the land is being refreshed, hearing the birds make their music during the day while crickets and locust serenade us at night; both given to us to see Him in it all.

The Bible tells us in Exodus that God told Moses to let the people know, "I am sent me." The great "I am" has control of everything. We need not worry. In the book of Matthew 6:25 it reads: *Therefore I tell you do not worry about your life, what you will eat or drink; or about your body what you will wear. Is life not more important than food, and the body more important than clothes?* That is to say animals do not worry, so why should we?

We are much more valuable than they, according to verse 25. It's very easy to worry when we see the sinful side of creation. We think that when bad things happen, they slipped past God's watchful eye.

Not so!

Remember He holds every star in place. He knows each hair on our head. He tells every lightning bolt where it should go. He is in total control. When there is a fresh blanket of pure white snow, be assured that not only is each flake different, He placed each snowflake specifically where it landed. Walking along the beach with each footprint pressed into the sand, He knows each grain. He cares for His creation. He gives us snapshots of Himself just so we can see Him through them. Look for the little things that make us see and let us know the big God we've got.

The other morning on my way to work, I saw my snapshot.

THE BEAR AND THE WHITE PIANO
By Todd Hogan

Not so very long ago, in a forest that splashed up against the faces of great mountains, there lived a grizzly bear with perfect pitch. Wild trees blanketed the mountains until they suddenly halted at their snow-capped peaks, while flower-strewn meadows dappled the valleys. The wilderness was shared by prey and predators, all seeking survival and continuation of their species.

The bear did not know he had perfect pitch. He considered it merely one more predatory advantage. The cries of wounded animals had timbre and tone which alerted him to the opportunity for a sustaining meal. He did appreciate birdsongs, which were melodic but not musical. Near the campsites where he scavenged for scraps, trash, and learned to open gates, he overheard TVs and could recognize the Wheel of Fortune notes, A♭-C-F-D, although he didn't know the names of those notes. Many of his instincts were ancient and rooted in survival, but he also had this newer instinct—that the sounds he heard could be beautiful, unusual, and meaningful, but they remained incomplete.

Like all bears, his hearing was as sharp as any dog's, and his sense of smell was five times keener than a bloodhound's. He could distinguish aromas three miles away. He now weighed over seven hundred and fifty pounds, slightly more than his brother. He valued the five claws on his front paws, each almost four inches long, useful for ripping apart tree trunks in search of food and hollowing out a den for the long winter's rest. With those claws, he could heft boulders like Atlas or delicately pluck individual berries from branches. Behind the sloping head sat a large, muscular hump which powered his paws to dig efficiently and swat dangerously. The fur on his body shaded to gray from deep brown as it grew, giving the bear a grizzled look. His brother's fur looked silver rising from cinnamon. He didn't know that the Latin name for his brethren and him was *Ursus arctos horribilis*, or he may have been offended.

The grizzly bear and his twin spent the first four years of their lives together. Their mother nursed, protected, and educated them until it was again time for her to mate. Then the two brothers ventured forth on their own. His brother, Silvertips, headed south to roam that territory, while he headed north. But each autumn, they held a reunion where the turbulent river cascaded over cataracts formed by ancient tectonic plates' upheaval. Flashing salmon swam the river on their final journey to spawn a new generation, then die exhausted. During these runs, predators lined the riverbanks, snagging the driven schools. The brothers ate the doomed salmon leaping the waterfalls. They devoured enough of thrashing fish to sleep comfortably until spring broke the forest's snowy cover. Then, ravenous, they would awake, bid each other goodbye, and return to his own territory and continue his search for sustenance.

#

The grizzly bear awoke one spring before his brother, eager to begin hunting. He picked up the fresh scent of a recent kill near the river. Probably a wolf pack had invaded his territory again. He believed that the wilderness was bountiful enough to provide for everyone, even more predators. For the last five years, he and the wolves had coexisted uneasily. His size and strength gave him the edge in most battles. But late last year, he saw that the packs were growing larger, and he worried that they might eventually be able to defeat him.

He cautiously followed the kill's scent, which led to a spot just above a six-foot waterfall. On the bank lay a mature elk, killed by wolves, but left unguarded. The bear sniffed the air again. The wolves were still in the area, but there were other kills further in the woods. As the bear investigated the elk carcass, he saw something he had never encountered before. It was a pair of metal jaws that had chomped on the elk's hind leg with enough force to have broken it. The elk would have been defenseless when the wolf pack arrived to end its misery.

The bear heard a mechanical vehicle, a jeep, bouncing through the forest. As the machine approached, the curious bear ambled into the forest growth to watch.

A tall man, defenseless, and a slender woman, also defenseless, left the jeep. The man, turning circles, used his wide-spread arms as he talked. The woman kept her arms tightly wrapped about her.

"And this is where the cabin will be. Right on the river! Its design will blend in with the trees, the rocks, and even the flow of the water. Like an updated Frank Lloyd Wright house."

"It's too remote. Isolated. I feel lonely already."

"You'll get used to the woods soon enough. The house will have satellite TV, internet. I'll import a library just for you. And, of course, I'll make sure you have a piano, a beautiful white piano. You'll be able to play and compose without anyone complaining. I can teach you to hunt."

"Oh, Leonard. Do we have to? I like our city apartment."

"This is our escape, okay? We don't have to stay here full-time, but just to get away."

"I'm not sure I want to get away, darling. I like an audience."

"Well, we both approved the blueprints, and I've made the down payment, and the construction will start next week. It'll be done by the middle of summer."

"I don't feel safe, Leonard."

"I'll make sure that no pesky wild animals will be anywhere within miles of this place. I've already started. The construction engineers laid metal traps around our land. Soon any curious beasts will learn to avoid our plot of land."

The man saw in the distance, near the river, the sprung trap with the dead elk. He turned the woman away from the sight before she could glimpse it.

"Oh, Leonard."

"Wait until you see our beautiful cabin completely built. You are going to love it!"

The wolf pack began to howl, an eerie wail that slid between the trees to echo along the river. The woman shivered. The man tensed, his small hands forming fists, his knees bent. He looked about him but saw nothing. He put his arms around her protectively.

"Come on. We should probably go."

The woman ran to the jeep. The man walked stiffly, looking around one more time. He tortured the gears, rocked the jeep backwards, and shifted into low. The jeep wobbled out the way it had entered.

After they left, the bear cautiously returned to the kill. Its bones still carried about two hundred pounds, enough to last at least two days. It would be a plentiful start to the new summer.

The bear ate his fill. Then he dug a small cave on the shore to bury the kill until his brother awoke and could join him. It took him until the sun was high, but at the end he had a mound that contained the remnants of the elk and overlooked the swift river.

The wolves howled again. This time the sound was closer.

#

He heard the snarls before he saw the yellow eyes of the pack in the shadows of the undergrowth. Their curled lips revealed sharp white stilettos. The bear's front teeth were long and good for ripping. His species' rear molars had evolved from razor sharp daggers to flat, sturdy, grinding surfaces, a consequence of no longer being carnivorous, but now omnivorous. He could eat anything, but preferred honeycomb.

The wolves crept forward, their shoulders hunched, their ruffled fur spiking. The bear spotted at least seven wolves, and he hadn't identified their leader yet. A few of the younger males led the advance toward the new mound on which the bear stood. He turned in circles to prevent being bitten from the rear. A large silver wolf, proudly waving her black tail with a brilliant white tip, observed regally from the edge of the clearing. The matriarch of the pack, she waited for the males to prove themselves.

The pack leader sprang forward from the trees into the clearing and suddenly halted. His head was high, his eyes bright. He surveyed the situation. A bear had tried to steal one of the kills they had claimed as their own. It didn't matter that there were four other elk with limbs broken by metal traps spread over the next few hundred yards, all had been killed by the pack. It was a matter of ownership. The leader yipped three times, two E*b*s followed by a D*b*, and the young wolves attacked.

The bear defended the high ground. He had no intention of hurting his fellow predators. He needed to assert his authority over the mound and protect his brother's meal.

The first few feints were easily defeated with swats from his powerful mitts. The wolves circled, positioned themselves, and waited, snarling. At another bark from the leader, two wolves attacked from different angles. The bear clobbered one, while the second latched fiercely onto the bear's inner haunch. The pain was intense, but not fatal. He kicked once, twice, a third time, before the wolf's bite ripped away.

Another wolf clambered onto the bear's back, using all his dexterity to remain high on the bear. He gnashed his teeth, trying to grab the bear's tiny round ears and rip them away. The bear laid his ears back and shook his head ferociously but ineffectually. Two more wolves took advantage of the bear's distraction to attack his rear and his flank. As he swung round, trying to fling off the sharp-toothed attackers, he saw the leader and his mate sitting together on their haunches, tongues lolling out of their maws, almost laughing. The bear stood on his hind legs and roared with pain.

He heard an answering roar. Silvertips burst from the forest and splashed across the river directly to the new mound. He showed no compassion for his fellow predators. With one mighty slap, he broke the back of one screaming wolf. His teeth caught the ear of the wolf that had been on his brother's back and ripped it and half the wolf's muzzle off. The other wolves froze in place, tails tucked, then darted towards the woods that stood behind the leader and his mate. The leader stood and slowly followed them, trailed by his mate. The brothers heard a single howl from the depth of the undergrowth.

Silvertips licked his brother's wounds as long as his brother permitted. Together they dug up the elk. They waited until their instincts to fight and kill had abated. Then they settled down to enjoy a most satisfying meal. After eating, the brothers swatted each other fraternally before leaving each other for the summer.

#

The grizzly bear traveled north, but not as far as he usually did. He kept close enough that he might return to watch the changes to his riverbank. By late spring, the foundation had been dug and poured. It happened that the home would extend over the original mound where the bear had buried the elk. It seemed an imposition, although the bear never claimed to own any property as such. Nevertheless, he was offended that the man laid claim to pieces of the wilderness to construct his own lair.

The next time the bear returned, he noticed the scent of wildflowers, honey, and citrus, which puzzled him. The man's lair was larger, fenced, with more than one level on which the man could promenade. One tier was floored with flat wood and protected by narrow wooden slats. It was on this raised platform that he spotted the woman again and recognized the source of the pleasant aroma.

The man was there as well, carrying a metal rod with a thick wooden stock. He and the woman were talking.

"Do you like the bedroom? It overlooks the valley on the east side. You can walk out onto the deck from our bedroom. Have coffee, tea, whatever right out here."

"It's lovely, Leonard. I couldn't have imagined."

"Have you seen the library? The entertainment area? When people visit, we can screen full-length movies for them, barbecue, serve liquor, set up a dance floor."

"Oh, Leonard. Do you really think anyone will come all the way out here to visit?"

The man took a deep breath. "Fresh air! Open spaces. Forests and our little buddies. It's a radical change from the garbage littering the streets of the city. Oh! And your piano is scheduled to be delivered this week."

"I'm going back to the city tonight. So I'll trust you to make sure it's acceptable."

"Acceptable? This is a classic antique piano. White. You're going to love it."

"Thank you, darling." She kissed his cheek. "I'm going to rest a little before leaving."

The man stayed out on the deck after she left, balancing the metal stick on his arm, sighting along its length. He bolted upright at something he saw, rebalanced the stick again, a large smile on his face. He closed one eye and squinted the other. Then the stick barked louder than any wolf he had ever heard, followed by a flash of light, a cloud of gray smoke, and the odor of intense fire. The man danced fast, tiny steps, then pumped the air with his fist. He drove a small tractor into the forest to retrieve his first kill.

An anguished howl began far away and was soon joined by others. The wails quavered up and down musically, and the bear noticed that the sounds produced modulated between dissonance and harmony. It expressed something that the bear didn't yet understand.

#

A few days later, the bear returned to the man's lair. He wanted to see the special white thing that the man had promised the woman. When a truck arrived mid-morning, three men helped to unload something taller than the man, broader than most mature tree trunks he had seen, and heavier than he and his brother combined. It was moved carefully, as if just tipping it might destroy it. It tinkled at times as it moved. Other times it grumbled.

The bear edged closer to the lair, next to the tall wooden fence that surrounded the place. Through the slats he could see through the sheets of frozen water that comprised most of some walls of this den. In one section of the room, there were shelves of multicolored books and comfortable chairs and a sofa. The three men muscled the white gift into a well-lit corner. The man observed, nodding his head and pointing occasionally. After the three men left, the man stayed to enjoy the sight of his gift. He lifted a wooden shelf in the middle of the white box, revealing a set of white teeth interspersed with groups of black sticks. Then the man put his hands on the teeth and touched them.

C.

It wavered in the air, beautifully resonant.

His hand moved again.

C-D-E-F-G-A-B-C.

The series of sounds thrilled the bear. The sounds were dependent upon the white box and controlled by the teeth!

The man closed the cover and left.

The bear edged away from the fence toward the forest. As he lumbered, he heard a menacing growl, and his shoulders hunched instinctively. He listened and pinpointed the sound. At the edge of the woods, he saw the pack leader pacing incessantly, growling in low tones, watching the shelf that the man had built. The bear looked back to where the wolf was looking. To his horror, he saw a silver wolfskin splayed against the wall of the lair, the snout tacked skyward. On a long pole attached to the deck, he saw an even more disturbing sight. At the top of the pole waved a wolf's tail, black with a brilliant white tip. He pitied the wolf's loss.

#

The bear kept his wandering to a minimum that summer, just so that he could stay close to the gift that had been given to the woman. He suffered a bit, since the only food he found to eat was limited to the grubs and insects he found by ripping tree trunks. He hadn't found any hives yet. The leaping elks and many of the larger deer and mountain goats had migrated, wary of the traps the man had set. Those traps were easily sniffed out by the bear and the wolf packs and easily avoided. Some of the wolves had learned to spring the traps using downed branches and small trees.

The wolf who lost his silver mate did not leave the area with his pack. The bear found the wolf pacing on each occasion he returned. The wolf studied the lair incessantly, his eyes searching for weaknesses in the lair's defense. Teeth marks on the wooden slats had tested their integrity. Random holes were dug around the perimeter, only to discover that the fence extended deep into the earth. The bear left him to his misery, while he cautiously approached the lair. He could hear the woman playing from across the meadow, but he preferred to watch her long, lean, jointed claws on the white teeth. He discovered that each white stripe and each black bar had a unique sound associated with it. No matter how many times it was scratched, the same sound pealed.

Some days he lay in the sun, blocked from the house, and listened to the way the woman could make several sounds at the same time. Three and four or more sounds together evoked an emotion, sometimes happy, sometimes sorrowful, always controlled by the woman.

One day he overheard them talking.

"It's not my fault people canceled. It happens."

"Face facts, Leonard. No one is going to come all the way out here to see your cabin in the woods. It's too far! It's inconvenient. And, it's dangerous."

"Dangerous? I've gotten rid of almost all of the predators who used to roam this ground. You're safe, dear. I'm the baddest predator in these parts now."

"Leonard, I'm lonely. How long do you think I can stay here just reading and playing the piano? I need company. And if they won't come to us, then we'll have to go back to the city."

"I thought you liked that piano. It's an antique. There are marks from the piano tuners that go back to the 1800's."

"It's an old upright, painted white over beautiful wood. It's quaint, but it's not what I'm used to. Couldn't you have invested in a decent concert grand piano? I need to work on my performance on a real instrument, not a toy."

"I priced a grand piano. It wasn't only the price that was prohibitive, but the transportation costs as well. And after all, what's the difference? This one has the same long strings as a grand piano, just in an upright position."

The woman groaned and turned on her heel to walk out of the room. Before she left, she, said, "If you can't hear the difference in pianos, then why am I even staying here with you? I need my audience. Someone besides that bear I see outside. At least that bear appreciates my playing." She slammed the door.

The man shook his head. He looked out the window, searching for the animal that listened to the woman's music. The bear met his gaze and felt uncomfortable, especially when the man grinned and narrowed his eyes. The bear trundled off deeper into the woods before the man could grab his metal stick.

#

For the rest of the summer, each time the bear visited the river, the man's lair was either empty or the man was there alone, drinking an acrid, muddy concoction and shooting his stick into the forest. The woman never returned, at least on any of the occasions that the bear was there. The wolf had stopped pacing, but he had not stopped watching. He had grown very lean and his pack had left him.

In the fall, the salmon began their run up the river's roiling waters. The annual run drew many predators, hoping to feed on the self-destructive yet life-affirming fish. The salmon were so single-minded about their mission that they didn't pause to eat. Anglers trying to hook them were disappointed. The successful fisherman acted like bears, snagging the salmon from the streams, lakes, and rivers. The grizzly bear knew his brother would soon return to their spot to fatten up for the winter, and he looked forward to seeing him.

As he waited, he also watched the man's lair, hoping that the woman might return one more time and send out the wonderful, measured sounds that issued from the large, white box. But he was continually disappointed. And one day, he saw that the man had used all of his strength and energy to move the white piano out to the area that contained his trash and garbage. He was ridding himself of the magical gift because he had no ability to unleash its potential.

The bear paced like the wolf had done while the wolf watched him with empathetic eyes. The bear rolled on his back and kicked the air. He snapped at butterflies. He growled in bursts that increased in ferocity.

Then he heard an answering growl. It was not angry or longing the way his own sound had been, it was an announcement. His brother was back and waiting near the edge of the water. The grizzly rolled over and began his loping run to greet his brother.

The met in the middle of the river, splashing and biting at each other's neck and ears. They stood upright; their long claws scratched the sides of the other. Salmon, undeterred by their presence, leaped upriver around them. The bears stopped and looked at each other. Silvertips looked good. He had put on more weight than the grizzly had this summer. Then again, the grizzly had spent much of his hunting time listening to music and hoping to see the woman again.

They positioned themselves atop the six-foot cataract, watching the fish resolutely try to make the seemingly impossible leap. The continuous roar of the falling water, churning just below them, added a sense of frivolity to their serious search for food. Again, and again the salmon tried. Eventually, some reached the top and continued on their journey. Some, though, reached the top only to meet a bear's jaws.

Suddenly, a loud bark echoed through the woods. The grizzly did not see the flash of light, but he did see a gray cloud, and smelled the intense fire. He saw the man dancing tiny steps rapidly and pumping his fist. The man took a large swallow from his brown bottle.

The bear turned back to his brother just in time to see his surprised look. Silvertips closed his eyes and fell forward. The force of the water propelled him, and he slid over the rocks arranged by ancient tectonic plates and into the churning whirlpool below. He burst out of that maelstrom and floated further downstream. His silver and cinnamon fur was surrounded by crimson water.

The man waited downstream with a long rope and a hook. He swung the hook twice before he snagged the dying bear and pulled him to shore. The man tied the bear to his tractor and dragged him into the fenced area.

The grizzly charged the bank of the river until the lean wolf cut him off. The anger and pain in the grizzly's eyes recognized the same emotions in the wolf, although the wolf seemed to have his emotions under better control. They stared at each other for a long minute, then scoured at the man's lair.

The bear knew he was powerless to save his brother, just as the wolf was powerless to bring back his mate. They watched the lair a while longer, then both ambled to the edge of the forest and lay down next to each other, waiting for night.

#

When night came, the bear roused himself while the wolf stood and shook himself from head to tail. Then they padded carefully to the fence that the wolf had found unassailable. The bear led them to the part of the fence near the trash area, where the piano had been moved. The wolf looked up at the bear, expectantly.

The bear stood on his hind legs and walked to the gate and its latching mechanism. The bear used his nimble claws to pick at the metal pegs, and within a few minutes he had unlocked the mechanism. He pulled the gate, expecting a squeak like the ones he often heard from the campground gates. But this gate was well-oiled and swung easily and silently on its hinges. He opened the gate as wide as possible.

He went to the piano and began to push it toward the opening. It was heavy, nearly impossible to move, but the bear found the strength to get it through the gate. The wolf waited nearby.

The bear pushed and pulled the white rectangular box until he reached the edge of the forest. The wolf found sticks and twigs to help the piano roll forward.

It was nearly dawn when the wolf and the bear succeeded in getting the white piano into the bear's winter den. He had the man's magical box. But it wasn't enough. This was, to the man, garbage. Then they both went back to the man's lair.

The gate was still open. Faint crimson tinted the morning sky as the deep azure of night retreated. On undulating stealthy paws, the wolf slunk around the open gate and padded into the man's enclosure. The bear waited.

The wolf yipped twice — Eb and Db. When the bear entered the enclosure, the wolf was poised to leap in front of a wide wooden door. The bear approached the door and with a single mighty slap, broke the door into splinters. The wolf hurdled the broken door and with a growl building in his throat, searched the lair for the man. The bear knew the wolf would find him. There was no need for him to wait.

The bear returned to his lair and examined the white piano. He used his paws to move a midsized boulder to the front of the piano, to use as a stool. Then he touched his claws on the white teeth. No sound came besides a clicking. He pressed harder. As he did, he heard a sound.

C.

He spread his skillet-sized paws over the teeth and tried again.

C-D-E-F-G-A-B-C.

He paused. Then he started to press the teeth in patterns of sounds that brought to mind events and people and feelings. After a long while, he played patterns of sounds that reminded him of the wolf's loss, the woman's loneliness, and his brother's death.

THE CLAN

By Alfredo (Freddy) Gutierrez

The day my young parents found out they were pregnant was the happiest moment of their lives. I was a complete surprise, but they loved me no less. My mother loved telling people how wonderfully scary the pregnancy was. She laughed loudly to herself every time she told the story. I could always tell she loved being a mother.

The first few years of my life were simple. My mother cared for me while my father went out to work. I loved her; she always did everything she could to keep me happy. She played with me, fed me, bathed me, and took me on walks. She'd put me to bed and read me stories every night. You know, the usual motherly stuff. But the one thing she could never do was figure out why I was so ... prone to accidents.

Poor lady, she nearly went mad trying to figure out how I kept falling into the arms of danger. She never knew how I rolled off my *secured* crib, or how that one time I ate half a string of Christmas lights. There were no cuts or bruises. She had no idea how I could jump out the car window and land on the busy highway without breaking a bone or even a scratch on my body. Or the time I stepped out of a moving rollercoaster ... I just wanted to fall. I wanted to feel the cart smashing into me at full speed. I wanted to feel every nerve in my body shock me out of its carcass before savagely throwing me back in. Yes, nine-year-old me wanted to die to see if I'd come back.

She shouldn't have jumped after me. My father shouldn't have jumped after her ... I loved my mother. I missed my mother.

How am I able to remember all that with such clarity you ask? I have no idea. But I remember everything, from the second I was born to a few moments ago when I lit myself on fire. I remember my mother sadly holding me against her chest seconds after birth. It was her wedding band that activated my lungs, the cold metal against my soft baby skin. It was so ... invigorating.

And here I am, 23 years later, naked and charred in an alley looking for the next hit, blow, clash, zap... anything that'll get my heart going or stopping. Whichever gets me closer to nihilism.

I don't really know why I am the way that I am. I don't know why Pete is the way he is. Or Mary. Or Lizzy. Or Carl. There's dozens of us and none of us know why we laugh in the face of death. Every. Day. But we do know we're all the same. We were all premature, born at six months. We're all 23, some for longer than others. And we cannot die.

We met one by one. Chance and our need for thrill brought us together. Dares and the lack of fear revealed what we were to one another. Brothers and sisters tied together by this incessant need for excitement. The closer to death, the more alive it makes us. And when we survive it, when we make it through, we immediately start looking for the next death - defying stunt.

I stayed in a dumpster for hours waiting for my skin to heal back to normal. Nobody wants to see a naked, crispy man waiting for the bus. Nobody wants to see a group of youngsters playing Russian roulette with a fully loaded gun in the park. And I know nobody wants to see a "daredevil" doing backflips on the ledge of a skyscraper.

The clan and I found out early on that people don't take kindly to us. But we get it, people are often afraid of what they don't understand. It took them decades to accept homosexuals and even longer to admit that transsexuals were not sick in the head. So we try to stick to the night to relieve our itching desires. They own the sun, but we roam the dark.

Through a crack on the dumpster lid I saw the passage of time. The streak of light revealed the progress of my healing. It never took less than an hour for our bodies to return to normal. I stared at the specks of dust and flies as they caught the light. I wondered what was next. I had tried nearly everything imaginable on my own and through dares. We were running out of excitement.

Later than night I met up with my best buds. We were happy pushing and shoving each other on the sidewalk. We laughed and hit each other in the balls. Every moment of our lives, whether alone or together was euphoric. Imagine never being hungry, never being sleepy or tired. Imagine the best buzz or high of your life. That precise moment in time when you feel like you can do anything you want, that feeling was every second of our lives and we loved it.

It didn't take long for Khalid to dare Abel to jump through a storefront window. Able began to spin in circles faster and faster and then boom! Glass flew everywhere. It sparkled with the streetlight before coating my eyeballs in short bursts of fire. I laughed hysterically as blood raced down my cheeks. Large shards stuck out from Abel's arms and legs. Khalid and Chino pulled them out and crushed them in their hands. The smiles on their faces were priceless and the pools of blood around them terrifying.

Soon we were all throwing ourselves onto other storefront windows, playing with the waves of glass like children in the rain. We loved it and our insides yearned for more. We ran through the streets jumping onto parked cars, smashing their windshields to pieces, laughing the entire time. Alarms and horns pulsated in our ears to the rhythm of our undying, unearthly desires. Behind us, a trail of glass, blood, and destruction reminded the world that those were the best of times.

Before dawn something unimaginable happened. We sat on the beams of a building under construction throwing a gun at each other. Russian roulette was one of our favorite pastimes.

"Click, click, nothing," we laughed.

"Click, click, nothing," we laughed.

"Click, click, nothing," we laughed.

"Click … click … BOOM!" we laughed as Khalid blew a hole in his head. A mist of blood dispersed through the air as he and the gun fell three stories down.

The guys and I jumped through the bones of the new building after him. We expected to see him laughing in a cloud of dust on the ground, but we didn't. We chuckled to ourselves as we approached him. The dust around us settled and revealed his *body*. His head was caked with bloody mud while life flowed out of him and soaked into the loose gravel.

"Khalid, you okay?" I muttered words I never thought I'd speak.

There was no answer.

An hour passed and we accepted that we would never hear Khalid's voice again.

As the sun rose, we diffused into the day; itching, laughing, wondering.

That night we met again, this time more of us but not all of us. We were jittery like addicts without a hit. We looked at each other, taking count of those missing. Some tapped the tips of their fingers while others paced back and forth mumbling. No one knew what was happening or why it was happening. Everyone looked at each other expecting an answer that no one could provide. Every now and then someone would burst out in laughter before falling lifeless to the ground, knife in hand. Gun shots rang through the walls of the dying alleys marking the inevitable count down.

"I gotta go," I said.

"Dude …" Chino said.

"This satisfies it," Abel finished his sentence.

"I can't, not like this," I replied.

The clan got smaller night by night. The excitement of waiting to die coursed through our veins as our lives regained normalcy. We became part of the 9-to-5 population who patiently awaited their turn.

THE FIRE PIT

By Mauverneen Blevins

Ivy Brunderson was a woman on the wrong side of her prime. Years of living with the wrong man had etched indelible lines into her once pretty face and erased all evidence of that young girl with a blonde ponytail and swinging hips. She lived on a farm a few miles out of town with her husband Jefferson. At least until he disappeared. Now she was taking things under control – feeding livestock, tending the garden, watching and eating what she wanted, when she wanted. Many evenings she took her plate outside, eating her dinner on the porch swing. Sitting at the table brought up too many visions of Jefferson pounding his fist onto the table, demanding she bring him something or other. She didn't need the flashbacks

On this particular afternoon, she was clearing some branches from a fallen tree, hauling them to a big pile and burning them when a car pulled into her drive.

A quick glance was all she needed to recognize the sheriff's car. She didn't stop working.

"Hey Ivy," the sheriff called to her as he stepped out of his car.

"Hey Bill. What brings you out this way?"

"Saw the smoke from the road and thought I'd check on you."

She nodded. "Everything's OK, just clearing up the last of that storm we had a while back."

"Looks like you could use some help with that. Too bad Jefferson ain't around."

"Is it?"

Now Ivy wasn't all that much for small talk. Especially when she had a job to do and right now her job was to get rid of that dead tree.

Sheriff Bill wasn't put off by her clipped reply. "Are you sure you haven't been able to think where he might have gone? We ain't had a single lead on that man."

"Hope you don't get none."

"And you have not heard from him at all?"

"Why would I? Man disappears off the face o' the earth you don't expect to hear from him."

"What will you do if he comes back?"

Ivy stopped what she was doing and gave that some thought. First off, she figured she'd probably have a heart attack.

"Don't rightly know. But I'd probably run off somewhere soon as I laid eyes on his sorry, miserable self." She went back to her work.

Bill wondered where she would run off to and why she hadn't run off before. Jefferson had abused her for years. Everyone in town knew it. It had crossed his mind at first that she may have done him in somehow, but there was no evidence of that. Not that they had looked too hard. Jefferson Brunderson had been known to not only beat his wife, but he'd also been known to have a little something going on the side a time or two and had been known to lift a cross hand there as well. He was particularly quarrelsome when drunk, which he was a lot of the time. Maybe he had decided to run off with one of his women. At least Ivy would have some peace.

"I am sorry for what you had to put up with that one, Ivy. Truly I am. But you know it didn't look good when you didn't report Jefferson missing."

"Didn't huh?" She looked directly at Sheriff Bill finally. "Did it look worse than that black eye he gave me? Or worse than the broken nose?"

Knowing there would be no answer, she turned back to her fire.

Bill looked down at his shoes to avoid her gaze, hitched up his belt and cleared his throat.

"That's some fire you got going there."

The tree had been a big one. An oak. A big storm had passed through several months earlier and the tree had been a victim. Before Jefferson had gone missing, he started cutting it up with a chainsaw. Ivy had decided to finish the job.

What Bill didn't know was that the fire was actually in a pit. A hole in the dirt, about four feet around. Jefferson had started on that, too, before he went missing. His plan was to butcher one of his hogs and barbecue it in the pit, invite the neighbors over. One day, in a drunken rage, he told Ivy he was digging her grave. He would put her in it and let her starve to death. He laughed as he told her. Thought it was funny.

"Well, Ivy," said Bill "If everything's under control here, I'd best get back to work. You need anything, you call. And let us know if Jefferson shows up."

"I'll be sure and do that sheriff," she replied, without turning around.

Sure, she'd call them. Just like she had called them the first time Jefferson beat her. Took them two days to get out and see if she was all right. Motherfuckers. She watched the patrol car turn around and head back down the drive toward the road before she threw another section of tree into the fire.

That last night he was out there digging and drinking, drinking and digging. And yelling at Ivy, who was in the house. He kept yelling for her to come and help him. She finally decided she would see what he wanted, just to shut him up and try to avoid getting beat for not coming out sooner.

"Bring me another bottle," he demanded, throwing his empty whiskey bottle into the hole he was digging. "This one's empty."

She did as he asked, hoping that he'd drink enough to pass out and leave her alone. It was a strategy that had worked for her before. Several times.

Ivy tossed him the bottle and when he went to catch it, he lost his balance, falling backward into the hole. She heard the sound of breaking glass. She stood in the dark a full five minutes, but there was no other sound out of the hole. No swearing, no yelling. No sound at all from Jefferson. She went and got a blanket from the house and went to sleep in the barn. Just in case he came to and decided to look for her.

In the morning, she crept over to Jefferson's hole in the ground. There he lay. Dead. She had poked him with the shovel to be sure. It was then that Ivy decided she needed to clean up that dead tree.

Ivy dragged another long branch over to the pit and pushed it on to the fire, watching the eager flames leap out and consume it.

Barbecue, she thought, and chuckled.

166

THE LEGEND OF PERKINS MACGHEE

By Kenneth Lee McGee

"Grandpa, can we walk over to the river?" Emmy asked. "It's not too hot and it's not super far to go since we're at Darby's."

"I suppose we can. Why do you want to see the river?" Grandpa asked as he finished his frosted mug of root beer.

"I just like to see it and watch the boats go by," eight-year-old Emmy answered. "Thanks for the root beer. It was yummy."

They returned their mugs and set out on their walk.

"I've been in there before," Emmy said pointing to a storefront.

"You have? When?" Grandpa asked noticing the iron bars over the windows of the pawnshop.

"Daddy brought me one time. He needed some money."

Grandpa shook his head. "That's no place for a child."

I saw an electric piano and asked how much it cost. Daddy said it was too expensive."

They continued along the commercial street for several minutes. Emmy would run ahead of Grandpa Colasanti and peer inside the shops.

"Who were you waving at?" Grandpa asked.

"That's the lady who does Mom's hair."

"Has she ever cut yours?" Grandpa asked.

"Mom let her trim it last year," Emmy answered as she ran her fingers through her long ponytail. "Just a little. She said I had split ends."

They crossed Broadmoor Avenue and turned to walk south.

"I know where we're going," Emmy said skipping ahead of Grandpa again. "There's a park over here where you can see the river."

A few minutes later they reached Pilchner Park.

"Can we go to the lookout and watch the boats?" Emmy

asked.

Grandpa paused to catch his breath and waved for Emmy to go ahead. She dashed along the uphill gravel path that wound through the trees. She stopped when she heard the loud horn of one of the tugboats that pushed the barges up and down the river. When Grandpa arrived at the top of the bluff, Emmy was standing on the bottom wooden rail of the fence to get a better view.

"There are three boats going downriver and I can see one over there waiting for them to pass," she said while pointing.

Grandpa gazed across the river, past the buildings of downtown South Hampshire to a bluff nearly a mile away.

"Do you know how the river got its name?" Emmy asked. "I've never heard of anything called Kinmundy before. It's a weird name."

Grandpa sat on the bench facing the river, removed his sweaty, baseball cap and ran a hand through his wiry gray hair. "According to the stories I've heard, it got its name from one of the early explorers who traveled up and down the river."

Emmy's eyes sparkled as she jumped down from the railing and sat next to her grandfather. "Tell me more."

He squinted while following a plane heading toward the airport on the other side of the city, rubbed his jaw for a moment and began, "Back in the late 1600s or so, this part of the country was pretty wild and unknown."

"Didn't they have maps?" Emmy interrupted.

Grandpa chuckled and said, "Not like we do today. Anyway, the only way people could get around was by canoe on the rivers, streams and lakes."

"Were there Indians?" she asked.

"I suppose so, because people have lived on the bluffs along the river for a long, long time. Sometimes they would exchange goods with the traders who were brave enough to get to know the natives. According to local legend, one of the traders was named Perkins MacGhee."

Emmy turned on the bench to face her grandfather. She put her hands under her knees and gazed into his eyes.

"He was a giant of a man. Several inches over six feet tall with long flowing hair under a hat made from beaver hides and

168

had a full bushy beard. He dressed in animal skins and spoke in a strange language."

Emmy inched closer.

"MacGhee came from Scotland to seek his fortune. No one knows just why or how he got to this area, but he traded with the Indians for several years. He would come and go up and down the river. He would camp along the far side of the river." Grandpa stood up and pointed to the east. "Can you see where the land rises?"

Emmy stood up and peered across the valley. "I think I can."

Thousands, or maybe millions of years ago, all that land was under a large lake. The river might have been a lot wider, too." He sat down and continued, "So this MacGhee decided to name the river after a place where he grew up. Loch Kinmundy. Loch means lake in Scottish."

Emmy stood up for a moment longer as two of the boats were passing each other.

"So he named this the Kinmundy River, and the name has stuck for all these years."

"Whatever happened to him?" she asked after sitting down.

Grandpa smiled and said, "That's where the story gets interesting."

Emmy's eyes sparkled again.

"According to the legend, one spring day MacGhee was heading down the river with a load of goods, and he kinda disappeared into the mist. Poof! He vanished into the fog. None of the locals ever saw him again, but they did find an empty canoe several weeks later. It had washed up on the island that's just before the big highway bridge."

"Did he drown? Did some mean people get him?"

Grandpa shrugged. "No one knows for sure, but they never found a body, or any of the goods he was carrying." Grandpa paused, and when he started again, his voice was just above a whisper, "This is where it gets spooky. Over the years, whenever there's a lot of fog and mist on the river, some of the boat captains swear they've seen a giant, bearded man in old-fashioned animal skins paddling a loaded canoe in and out of the mist."

"Are you making that up, Grandpa?" she asked sitting up and crossing her arms over her chest.

He waved a finger and said, "I'm not making it up. That's the true story of how the river got its name and the legend of Perkins MacGhee."

THE SPANISH SISTER

By Annette Gonzalez

She was so small—like a tiny, white rectangle against the grandness of the building next to the *Catedra de Malga*. I stood there staring at her in her white nun's habit. She had come out onto the balcony, floors above me, but only part way. She stood half-way in-between the curtains and the outside, almost as though she did not want to be seen. If not for the starkness of her white clothes, I would have surely missed her. She watched as the orchestra prepared for the baroque concert on the steps of the ancient cathedral.

Sarah, my traveling companion, tapped me on the shoulder calling my attention to a man who was selling flowers. We smiled as we'd seen a statue of a man selling flowers just like this earlier today. It was as if the statue had come to life to be in this moment.

Returning my gaze to the balcony, my white nun is gone. I stared for a while, hoping for her return, but she does not appear. Perhaps Mother Superior called her back inside. Perhaps her apprehensive visits to the balcony had been only moments stolen from her duties.

It was nine in the evening and the Spanish sun was setting. Parishioners filled the cobblestone area in front of the church. Periwinkle dresses and navy suits. Sarah and I in our casual American clothes.

The first couple of chords of Handel's "*Alleluia*" rang out making my skin tingle, calling me to attention. I glanced upward toward her balcony in hope that this grand sound would summon her back. How wonderful to be a Spanish sister in this place, where each small town boasts at least one grand cathedral, once a Moorish temple. This place should indeed have Spanish sisters in white.

White, the purest of all colors; it stands alone. When blended with other colors, it weakens them, lightens and tames with its own strength, demanding the acknowledgement of its presence. White cloth upon which any discoloration stands as dirty, soiled. The white habit, pure in its own virginity, uninfected by color or imperfection. She wears it for Him; she is one of His brides, and do not all brides wear white? These brides, never deflowered, never fouled by the hands of mortal men, to be touched, caressed and wooed only by Christ, God, Himself. They alone are worthy of wearing the whitest white.

At the fourth *alleluia*, she reappeared, this time stepping full onto the balcony, leaving the curtains swaying behind her. Leaning her body up against the railing, she draped her hands tenderly across it. The song progressed and a gentle breeze began blowing as the phthalo blueness of the night enveloped us. I could see her raising her head to the heavens as though beckoning her love to come to her on this most perfect night.

"Here is your bride, here in the celebration of *your* song, here is your bride in the purest white. *Take her.*"

The wind blew faster and harder, blowing the skirt of her habit against her thighs, the music bounding, the bass notes coming on stronger now. The light strings entering the chorus and leading to each of the *alleluias* and pushing the sleeves of her habit close onto her arms, caressing them. Her veil blowing in the wind of each note like wild Venus hair, her head held high giving herself onto His music; *to Him.* Each alleluia a stroke of his hand. God's own thunderbells bouncing off these cathedral walls.

The music stops, my gaze breaks. I want to see her in the afterglow of it all. She is gone. Only the flutter of the curtains remains.

THE WORD, THE FLESH, AND THE DEALERSHIP

By Todd Hogan

A crescendo of whispers began as Father David Ruiz left the lectern. The chatter delayed the offertory hymn. Father Ruiz settled himself to await the presentation of the gifts. From the back of the church, applause began until it seemed everyone was clapping. He chose to take it as a token of respect after his twenty-seven years with St. Thomas.

After the noon Mass, a few parishioners stopped to wish him well.

"We'll miss you, Father. You give the shortest sermons," said Mrs. Olivia Kittrell, one of the oldest members of the parish.

The priest smiled. "I've learned — the shorter the homily, the fuller the collection basket."

Mrs. Kittrell regarded him through her thick glasses. "You have all the right answers, too."

They both laughed.

"What about your legacy, Father? Maybe it's just my age, but one must consider how one will be remembered."

"That's just vanity, Mrs. Kittrell."

"What about your new hall for drunks and drug addicts?"

The priest winced. "Well, it's no secret I've had trouble drumming up support for the Family Center. I expect AA and NA and others could meet there, sure, but also Grief Counseling, Marital Counseling."

"I'd rather contribute to a new gym for the parish," A booming voice announced.

Packy McGuire stood a head taller than the priest. He had the build of an ex-football player who still played tennis. McGuire gave the priest a hearty two-handed handshake that rattled his loose wristwatch. His bright, resonant voice could be heard throughout the emptying parking lot.

"It won't be the same, David. When're they moving you out?"

"A few more weeks."

"We'll miss ya, pal. You'll still do my Sally's wedding, right?"

"Your daughter's getting married?" the priest teased, causing McGuire's jaw to drop a moment.

"What did you have to promise to get her to tie the knot?" asked Mrs. Kittrell.

"Cut it out, you two," McGuire laughed. "Be nice, Olivia, or I'll seat you at the children's table. It's going to be spectacular, 'cause she's my baby girl. Even Kevin came back this summer from Boston for the ceremony. You remember Kevin?"

"Of course. Wonderful young man. It was probably wise he left the seminary."

"The Church lost a so-so priest, but I'm gaining a world-class salesman. He's graduated now from Boston University."

"Is Kevin here today?" Father Ruiz asked.

"No, no. He probably went to an earlier Mass. Who am I kidding? He didn't go to Mass. I'm worried about the boy, David. He's turning his back on all religion. He refused to be a groomsman for Sally's wedding. He doesn't want to participate in 'a fairytale farce.' And Katie asked him to be the godfather for her newest and he won't. That's not like him, you know, Father?"

"Young people go through times of doubt, in my experience."

"He's so graciously agreed to attend the baptism today and the wedding coming up. But he told me he wants to go back to grad school. To grad school! He wants his MBA! Nothing against education, but I'm ready to hand him the reins of one of the most successful car and truck dealerships in the Midwest. Most young men would kill for that opportunity."

"It can't hurt to be a little more prepared for the business world, can it?"

"I had a high school diploma when I started. It hasn't hurt me. Kevin wants answers. There are no pat answers for the kind of questions that the business world throws at you every day."

"The business world be intimidating. It seems so unforgiving."

McGuire scoffed. "The business world forgives Success anything."

Mrs. Kittrell tapped her foot and cleared her throat.

174

"I'm sorry, Mrs. Kittrell. Were we ignoring you?"

She shook her head, but her lips were pressed together tightly. "I just wanted to know, will we get a foreign priest now? I can barely understand some of the visiting missionary priests."

"I don't know, Mrs. Kittrell. I am going to miss you."

McGuire took her arm and tucked it into his. "Come on, Olivia. Let me give you a lift home in a brand-new Lincoln Navigator."

She giggled next to him. "Well, maybe just this once."

McGuire turned back to the priest. "Kevin could use your advice. If you see him. Find out what's his problem. He won't open up to me yet. At least he respects you. I'd appreciate it."

"Goodbye, Packy. Goodbye, Mrs. Kittrell."

"The baptism is today, Father. He won't be a godfather, but Kevin will be there."

As they left, Father Ruiz thought that the miscommunication between McGuire and his son would be perfect matter for a new Family Center.

#

That afternoon, Father Ruiz took time to observe three baptisms performed by his lay deacon. He saw three babies and their parents, ready for the ceremony. In the back of the church, he saw a young dark-haired man in a sports coat and tie, sitting in a pew with his arms crossed.

"Hello, Kevin. Which baby belongs to you?"

"Not funny, Father."

"Mind if I sit here?" Father sat down, forcing Kevin to scoot a little to the middle.

"Your church. I may have to leave early. I'll stay as long as possible."

"I understand. Is that your sister on the left?"

"Yeah, Katie. That's Dylan, her husband. That other kid is their first, Joey. He's a handful. Don't worry. He was baptized about four years ago."

Katie was surrounded by the McGuire family including her father Packy and Dylan's family, about twenty-five people all told.

"I don't know the other parents up there," Kevin said. "The first looks too old to be baptizing three children, and the other looks like a single mom. I should feel sorry for her, but actually I'm kind of in awe."

Father Ruiz nodded. "I know both families. That older couple were approaching forty and were desperate for a child. They had negotiated the adoption of two children from Columbia. When they flew down to pick them up, the children's mother had recently delivered a third baby who was deaf. The couple adopted all three children on the spot. They're beginning to learn sign language."

"You're promising them a special place in heaven, aren't you, Father?"

"I'm praying for them."

"Tell me about the other family."

Those godparents cradled the baby tenderly. The mother, dressed in a satiny teal dress, stood stiffly next to the godmother, her chin held unnaturally high. "She's a single mother who works from home. That's her sister and brother-in-law standing in as godparents. I knew her growing up at St. Thomas. She drifted from the Church, so I'm pleased to see her here today."

The lay deacon introduced himself and the families on a microphone pinned to his surplice. The church loudspeakers echoed so that the words could not be heard clearly, plus the deacon spoke a little too fast.

Kevin sat forward in the pew, his hands between his knees.

"You have a problem with the ceremony?" the priest whispered.

Kevin looked at him. He shook his head. "You don't get it, Father. They all are here only for the photo opportunity. After this, Katie and Dylan are hosting a baptismal party at one of the pizza places. That's where the real celebration takes place. They think of the Sacrament of Baptism as a kind of spiritual tattoo, zap! marking new souls entering Christian territory."

"You have a better idea than Baptism?"

"Of course not. They're satisfied that the deacon will promise salvation with a small dose of Holy Water and a dab of chrism. It's just that a deeper commitment and understanding of this ceremony would be nice."

"The deeper commitment and understanding of salvation will come later, after they have matured. This ceremony isn't perfect, but it's a good start, don't you think?"

The deacon intoned the Baptismal vows. "Do you renounce Satan? And all his works? And his empty promises?" Because of the muddied speaker system, no one could understand the words, so the deacon answered for the children. "I do renounce him. I do renounce them. I do renounce them."

Joey had a defiant smile on his face. One small clear voice answered the final question in the negative.

"I don't!"

His father Dylan began to giggle, then laugh, to the point he had to leave the church, carrying the boy.

"In the past the Church would have burned my nephew at the stake," Kevin said.

"We're lucky the Church is more forgiving these days."

"My father might say too forgiving. I've got to go. I have to plan my entrance at the pizza party."

"My door is always open, Kevin."

Packy McGuire caught the priest before he left the Church. "I saw you talking with Kevin. How did it go?"

"He'll be at the pizza party. That's some headway, I suppose. Let's give him some space."

"Something's eating him. He won't tell me. Did he mention a girl he was seeing for a while back East? She's no longer in the picture, but I think she may have done a number on the poor kid. What do you think?"

"He's figuring things out, I think. Let's give him time."

"Not too much time, okay, Father?"

#

Sally McGuire's wedding day arrived a few weeks later with the pomp of a royal affair. She had eight bridesmaids, eight groomsmen, a young flower girl, and an even younger Joey as ring-bearer. The wedding planner commandeered the church, festooning it with ribbons and flowers to achieve her goal of providing a visually stunning backdrop for the ceremony. The videographer had cameras set at the corners and in the back, as well as two hand-held cameras for more candid shots. Outside, they tested the drone camera to be sure it would capture the bridal parties as they arrived at St. Thomas.

Packy McGuire made a last-minute check of the church, checking the work of the wedding planner.

"I've got this, Mr. McGuire," she said to him, guiding him toward Father Ruiz, where she left him. Then she yelled into her headset, "Where are my yellow drumsticks? The freakin' florist promised to deliver them by now. Where are my craspedia?!"

McGuire took a moment to show Father Ruiz his new tuxedo.

"Looks nice, Packy, but you're not playing baccarat at Monte Carlo, you know."

"I've got another daughter and a son, so I to hope to use it again, eventually."

"I've not seen the groom at St. Thomas before. Are you sure he's even baptized?"

"He's a good kid, but what do you call it? 'Questioning.' Questioning everything. But Sally's in love. What's a father to do? Sally's already hinted I should give him a job."

"And you will."

"I might. He better work out better than the other clowns she's begged me to hire."

The two men looked at each other.

"Twenty-some years, eh, Father?"

"Twenty-seven. Where does the time go? Everything looks beautiful. I love the flowered trellis at the entrance to the narthex. Uh, oh. The wedding planner is screaming at someone on her headset. You better finish checking everything over. I've got the ceremony covered."

Packy nodded and trotted off.

Father Ruiz let the wedding ceremony play out in its minutely structured format. He was uncomfortable at the careful way the Sacrament of Marriage was co-opted, all on a time schedule: the music, the gowns, the way the relatives of the groom and the bride were led down the aisle, the presentation of flowers, the prayers that were said before the Virgin Mary's statue but were probably just one more photo op. The Mass was no longer the heart of this production. It had been streamlined. They had scheduled a picture-taking opportunity at a popular open-air flower garden. It needed to be completed in time to get to the reception, too. As a result, Father's Ruiz's speaking part was rather limited.

The bride and groom both read their own statements, joined by the best man and maid of honor who had trivial, romantic things to say. Father Ruiz began to wonder if he would get an opportunity to address the couple or the congregation.

So, his words to the couple were simple.

"Remember: Your marriage will grow in proportion as you show love. You can overcome any challenge, any disappointment, any problem, any sin with love."

He doubted they heard him. Their eyes darted constantly side to side, looking for the next bit of theatre to complete.

He blessed the rings. He said the sacred words; they repeated their vows. They now were bound before God and the state by this sacrament. They kissed. The congregation applauded, whistled, and laughed. The strain of the performance was starting to wear on everyone. Sally's smile was tightly fixed, perspiration showed at her forehead, and there were tears in her eyes. When Father Ruiz's official duties were completed, the couple bustled out of church into the luxury cars provided by Sally's father, trailed by the camera-mounted drone.

The thought occurred to Father Ruiz that the Church would likely never see them again.

#

At the reception, Father Ruiz was seated with Packy McGuire's parents and their old friend, Mrs. Kittrell, who looked uncomfortable and was feeling under the weather. Their table, one of over eighty for the guests, lay on the periphery, not far from the hallway, but removed from the band, the noise, and the head table. The reception bubbled with relatives, friends, and customers, dressed in shiny suits or short dresses. When the live band took a break, the ping of glasses, shouted conversations, and the rattle of metal chairs on the parquet floor contributed to a din that made it nearly impossible for Father Ruiz to hear the table conversation.

Sally's mother made the rounds, briefly stopping at their table. She looked tan, nervous, and exhausted. Her latest annulment, her second counting the one from Packy, had not been granted yet. She put an arm around Father Ruiz and tried to shout near his ear before he cut her off.

"I'll pray for you, but I have nothing to do with granting annulments. I'm sure you'll be free to remarry in the church soon, my dear."

"In the church," she said out of the side of her mouth, waving to someone at another table as she left.

"Ah, she drinks, you know," said Mrs. Kittrell, herself a little thick-tongued.

The evening progressed loudly. Father Ruiz was the last guest at his table. He stayed because he knew he would miss these people after his transfer.

He felt a light touch on his shoulder.

"Hey, Father," a young man's voice shouted above his ear. He stood and grabbed Kevin McGuire's hand. They eased over into the hallway, where the noise was marginally softer.

Kevin not only stood a head taller but also wider than the priest. His tuxedo cummerbund accentuated his athlete's waist. He hadn't spared his woody, tangy cologne. He checked the hallway at both ends, then leaned closer to the priest, hesitant. He straightened without speaking. Father saw indecision on his face. His mouth tightened. He leaned forward again.

"Sorry to hear you're leaving, Father."

Father Ruiz nodded his acknowledgement. He studied the young man quickly.

"So, what did you study in college?"

Kevin shrugged. "I got a business degree. Economics, Accounting."

The conversation lagged as the priest waited for the boy to overcome his reticence. Kevin seemed to wrestle with the words he wanted to say, but he finally said nothing.

"Your sister Sally makes a beautiful bride."

Kevin smirked. "This is all Dad's doing. She was happy just living together with Tony. I talked to her and I couldn't convince them to get married. You talked to her. After two years, Dad finally told Sally that he would give her a down payment on a house if she and Tony would make it legal and not just live together."

Father Ruiz chuckled. "It seems money is a better persuader than you, me or love."

"I would hate to believe that," Kevin said, looking away.

"Now, you never told me. What did your father promise you, Kevin? Was the decision to leave the seminary entirely yours?"

Kevin shook his head. "You're wrong there, Father. It wasn't like that."

"I respect your decision, Kevin. Although, in all my years, I've never had anyone become a priest. I had no expectation that you would be the first. I'm glad you discovered your business vocation before you went too far along the priestly path."

"I had to face facts, Father. I can't be like you. I enjoyed...other people too much. Becoming a priest was the answer for you. I haven't found an answer."

"Is that why you're leaving to get your MBA?"

"It's one reason. Maybe I'll find what I need."

His father's clear resonant voice echoed in the hallway. Kevin stiffened, his eyes darting.

"Kevin, Kevin! Your sister Mary Fran needs someone to dance with her. Why don't you leave Father Ruiz and me to talk?"

McGuire clapped his son on the shoulder and gave him a slight push in the direction of the dance floor. He was careful not to spill his own cocktail. Kevin nodded to the priest, a gesture the priest took to mean, "Gotta go," or "We'll talk more."

McGuire put his arm around the priest's shoulders. "Did you talk to him, David? Did he open up to you?"

"We talked a little. He's looking for an answer. He hopes he'll find it with an MBA."

"He's a good boy, Father. He's got a lot to offer."

The priest slipped McGuire's arm. "To your business, you mean?"

"Father, look. He's decided not to be a priest. We both know that. Let's face facts. Life goes on."

"Too bad. He would have been a good one."

McGuire gulped his seven and seven. "Businesses need ethical leaders, too. Look. I sell the most cars of any Midwest dealership. My father built the business up for me. I'm building it up for my kids. But you see the kind of young man Sally, Katie, and Mary Fran attract."

"They are lovely young ladies, Packy. You should be proud of them."

"Oh, I am, I am. They just could be a little more choosy. Kevin, too. You can never tell him this, Father."

Father Ruiz looked at McGuire inquisitively.

"Kevin was hot and heavy with some girl back East. That's the reason he wants to get his MBA, I was sure of it. He'd go back there, she'd trap him, and goodbye everything I've built up. Eventually, I made a payment to her to make her forget all about the boy. It was substantial, but worth it, I think. But you can never tell him. I don't think he would appreciate it at his young age. Maybe when he's older, he'll have a more worldly view."

A snare drum roll and happy, excited shrieks alerted everyone that Sally was preparing to toss her wedding bouquet. Mary Fran elbowed her way to the front of the crowd of other beautiful, hopeful young women, as much to be photographed as to snare the bouquet. McGuire excused himself to get a better look at the festivity, while the priest watched from the hallway.
#

Near the end of the summer, Father Ruiz leaned uncomfortably in the confining confessional on a Saturday shortly before he would be leaving St. Thomas. His thumb and forefinger stretched the skin over his forehead even more tightly. He prayed over his priestly power and responsibility to forgive the sins he heard confessed. Nothing compelled him to forgive the peccadillos he heard confessed, and yet he would. His parishioners viewed the Sacrament of Reconciliation as a metaphysical car wash. Soiled souls in, cleansed souls out, just for the asking.

A young man's voice, soft-spoken. Pungent aftershave. "Bless me, Father. My last confession was…It's been a while."

"What would you like to confess?" Based on the youthful voice, the priest assumed the confessor had probably been caught in an embarrassing situation—a theft, adultery, substance abuse. Confession was part of his twelve-step recovery program.

"I've lied, missed going to Mass, and used some pretty foul language…"

Father Ruiz rubbed his eyes behind his rimless wire glasses. Nothing extraordinary to bring the lad to his knees yet. He waited. The boy was winding up to pitch the big sin, the blot on his eternal soul.

"…I've slept with a girl at college. More than once. Often."

"I see. You realize that relations outside of the sacrament of marriage are wrong. And have you made a firm resolution to sin no more?"

He paused. "It's not that, Father. I believe that what we did was beautiful. We loved each other. That's not a sin. It can't be."

Father Ruiz had placed the voice, surprised that he hadn't recognized Kevin McGuire immediately. He was not surprised at the young man's sin, though. It was almost a rite of passage for university students to enjoy sex.

"Then, I don't understand what you're here to confess."

"You're the priest, not me. You're supposed to know what all the sins are. All I know is that things are different now. I loved her and she loved me. But we haven't talked or seen each other since…for a while now. She won't answer my calls or texts or emails. She refuses to see me."

"Son, how well do you really know this woman?"

"That's pretty obvious, isn't it?"

"I suppose so. Let me ask you. Are you suggesting that I reach out to her? That she might like to come in for counseling? Would you both want counseling?"

"I don't think so, Father. She's from back East, and she's not Catholic."

The priest imagined him shuffling behind the screen, changing posture, maybe shrugging his shoulders. He knew there was more that the young man had not told him.

"So, how do you feel now?"

"It scares me, Father, what we became, what we did together."

It was warm in the close darkness.

"What did you do, Kevin?"

"Father, we went out for my whole senior year. She was amazing. But I got her pregnant." He paused before continuing in a desperate voice. "We couldn't keep it. She still lives with her parents, and I still depend on mine. We talked about her procedure. It's perfectly legal. It's her constitutional right. Between her doctor and her. That should do it, don't you think?"

Father Ruiz's shoulders sagged, and he bowed his head. This young man's confession reminded the priest how he had failed his congregation again. He felt particularly chagrined and ineffective because he once had such high hopes for the young seminarian.

"Then she had an abortion. I drove her there and I gave her the money for it. But we haven't talked since then." Kevin let out a deep breath, rushing to the formulaic ending. "For these sins, I'm heartily sorry and vow to sin no more."

The priest knew that forgiveness was expected at this point, together with an appropriate penance.

"You could always pray for that child, Kevin."

The voice strained to be forceful within the confines of a whispered conversation. "But it wasn't a child. Christ. It was, you know, nothing. A peanut."

"So, no sin if it's a nothing, is there?"

"Why couldn't I convince her? Why couldn't I change her mind?"

"I don't know, Kevin. I don't know. I do know that there are situations and decisions that are outside your control. There are problems and challenges and troubles that God sends to each of us."

"So I failed His test? Great! Now what?"

"I sometimes think God sends us challenges knowing that we will fail. Why? I don't know. Perhaps to knock us off our smug pedestals, to remind us that we are not in control of the world, not matter how clever and powerful we think we've become. Only God is."

"I dream about him, that nothing, my nothing, my peanut." He swallowed. "Who would he have been? And who is he now?"

Father Ruiz asked the next question carefully, like probing a wound. "If your peanut were real...this somebody you dream about...What does that make you?"

No answer, no noise came immediately from behind the wire mesh. The penitent on the other side might have bolted. Father cocked his ear to hear the answer when it came, a single, disembodied sound, spoken as though it had been dropped from a steeple.

"Alone."

Not the word Father Ruiz had expected. He sighed, disappointed with the young man and with himself. He strained to see the face of his dangling watch. The small room seemed even quieter, darker.

"What do I do now, Father?"

"I'll give you your penance and your sins will be forgiven."

A strained whisper. "My life's got to change. It's horrible. I feel horrible. I'm lost."

The priest straightened in his seat, closed his eyes and lowered his chin to his chest.

"I know, Kevin."

"Father..."

"What?" The priest sounded abrupt, even to himself.

"Nothing, Father. Nothing."

Father Ruiz ran through his catalogue of admonitions gained over years of hearing other people's sins confessed. None seemed appropriate for this suffering young man.

"Kevin," he spoke quietly, "say three Our Fathers, three Hail Marys. That will do it; it's enough. Make a good Act of Contrition. Then, Kevin, your sins are forgiven." He listened for Kevin to begin his prayer.

"Do you really believe that, Father?"

A question like that. Twenty-seven years in a parish sometimes seemed too short a time to reach anyone, to make any impression. He sighed quietly and hoped Kevin didn't hear him.

"Yes," he said. "I believe it. You can start fresh with your carwash clean soul."

"Thank you, Father." Kevin whispered so quietly that the priest almost missed it.

#

Old Mrs. Kittrell passed suddenly on a Sunday. Her funeral was held on Friday, one of Father Ruiz's last official acts for St. Thomas. Most people viewed a funeral as a social obligation, a chastened bon voyage, a gathering to witness the last leg of the journey. They prefer not to have to confront death's cold reality. When death touched a family, a funeral suddenly became a personal question, a fundamental examination of existence. His sacred duty was to help his flock believe in a world beyond the frailties of this one.

He saw Packy McGuire at the service, which was not surprising. He also saw Kevin McGuire at the service, which was surprising. Kevin talked to each of the mourners, offering his condolences. He participated. Even his father looked impressed.

The priest led the group in prayers that were familiar and sounded comforting when murmured over someone's loved one. He blessed the body and the family and prayed for the people gathered. Some wept over Mrs. Kittrell, the one they had lost. Some pondered the ambiguity of passing. Others reasoned it was her time.

Following the service, Father Ruiz joined her family for lunch in a private room at an Italian restaurant. He liked the way sharing a meal helped the grief healing begin. Mrs. Kittrell's three children and seven grandchildren survived her. Not a close family anymore, few are, but they would miss her in the weeks that followed.

Packy McGuire cornered the priest before he left the luncheon. "You know, you ever want to give up this priest gig, I would hire you in a heartbeat. You're a born salesman. It looks like you've turned Kevin around. I don't know how, but I'm grateful. I'm even thinking about a generous donation to your Family Center."

"Kevin's not going to study for his MBA in the fall?" This was the first the priest had heard of it.

"I've seen a change in him, Father. It's your doing. Anybody that can get people to part with their hard-earned wages by promising the great unknown would be a superstar selling shiny new automobiles. Any time you want a job, you come to me, Father."

"That's not my vocation, Packy. It may not be Kevin's vocation yet, either."

"David, Kevin will run a good dealership. He'll take it regional or national, I don't know. Anything is possible. I do know that the car business is changing, and it'll take bright young people to keep up with the market."

"Give him some time, Packy. He'll do what's right."

McGuire shook his head. "I don't have time, David."

"Sure, you do. You're a still young man, not an old gasbag like me."

"No, David. No, I haven't. I haven't told anyone but you now. I got the Final Recall. The Big C. In my pancreas. Of course, I'm not giving up. There are new treatments every day and I know at least a dozen people who are in remission. So..."

The priest put his arm around his friend. "I'm so sorry, Packy. Anything I can do?"

"Convince Kevin to take over the dealerships might help. Otherwise, do your prayer thing."

"Packy, have you tried just talking to your son? This is the kind of information he should have. In fact, your whole family should know about this."

"No. Not yet, Father. Not yet."

#

His farewell party lasted from two until five on Sunday afternoon in the old gym. Father Ruiz spent the time tentatively hugging older parishioners and gently coddling younger ones. Those who came, moved through the receiving line rapidly, wished him well, and then left. Not many stayed the whole time—a few original parishioners with nothing else pressing that afternoon, two women who organized the event, and Kevin McGuire.

Father Ruiz stood at the far corner of the old school gym, holding cold coffee in a Styrofoam cup. A painted banner posted beneath the scoreboard read "Farewell Fr. Ruiz — Thank You for 20+ Years!" The scorer's table still held thirty-two pieces of white sheet cake and two silver urns half-filled with coffee. The organizers had expected a larger turnout.

Kevin waited until almost five before approaching the priest. When he did, he looked him in the eye.

"It's too bad you're leaving, Father."

"New parishes need experienced priests. Even old ones like me." He looked for a place to dump the bitter coffee until Kevin offered to take it and found a trash can.

Packy McGuire's bright, resonant voice carried through the gym. He shook hands and joked with the few still left, recognizing friends, customers, and potential customers. As usual, he was dressed as handsomely as an NBA coach. He eventually reached Father Ruiz and extended his large palms in his typical two-handed shake, rattling his wristwatch.

"Good luck to you, Father."

"Hello, Packy, thanks for coming."

"After all these years together? I had to, Father. Well, what do you think of my Kevin here?" The father and son standing shoulder to shoulder formed a wall that towered over the slender priest. Kevin slipped his father's grasp with a juke.

"He's not the same altar boy who came up through the grade school, is he, Father? I'm hoping the car dealerships appeal to him now."

Kevin shook his head. "I don't think we should count on that, Dad. I'm still considering the priesthood."

McGuire stopped talking and looked at his son, sadness in his eyes. Then he shot Father Ruiz an angry look. "What kind of bullshit have you been selling my boy?"

"It's my decision, Dad, nobody else's. You've got to trust me to make my own decisions, okay?"

"Packy, have you talked to your son? Have you told him?"

"I was relying on you, David. I see I was mistaken."

McGuire pasted on his best salesman's smile and clapped Kevin on the back. "We'll talk later, son. Well, Father, I think we have to run. Great to see you, and good luck with your new parish. Oh, and I decided I'm funding a new gym for the parish, the best gym in the diocese."

They shook hands again, not quite as warmly as before.

Kevin kept his head bowed.

Father Ruiz told Kevin, "You know, becoming a priest was not part of your penance."

"Then why does it feel like it is?"

"Your father is going to need you, Kevin. Trust me. Talk to him."

"He'll never change. That's what everyone loves about him. That's not me."

"He's dying, Kevin. He needs you."

"Lots of people are dying. Maybe lots of people need me. Maybe they need someone who can sell them God more than a feature-filled SUV. You should know, Father. You made this choice."

"I trust your judgment, Kevin. But you owe your father a conversation explaining your decision, don't you think? And he owes you one, too. If you can't speak to him, it will be difficult to preach to a congregation. Believe me."

The lights in the old gymnasium clicked off. It was time to leave.

11566 S. S. "ROOSEVELT." PASSING THROUGH STATE STREET BRIDGE, CHICAGO, ILL.

THIS IS ENTIRELY PREVENTABLE
or
STILL MISSING IN HICKORY CREEK

By S. Houk

I have so mismanaged my life
there is no point doing yoga now.
How do I start?
I won't buy anything.
I'll just sit on the floor
and stretch my world.
I'll stretch past the people
who would do me harm.
I'll stretch a long way past them.
I'll stretch 'round the corner of
Hey! Hot Dog
for some root beer in a frosted glass.
Darkly in a frosted glass?
Bubbly with some ice cream.
To float.
I don't need to see me.

I need to see the lip
of the baseball stadium,
a barge under the bridge
opened up in prayer
to the heavens:
come down and fish.
Fish out the boy
who tried to outrun a train.
Tell him it's not too late
to do yoga.
Watch the train from a high bank.
Watch it rumble over the draw bridge.
Where you aren't.
Your arms to heaven.
Your feet on ancient pilings

THIS WORLD IS

By Holly Coop

A world that has lost its good taste
A world that has lost sight
A world in desperate need
To an end to its many a plight
A world craving *salt*, a world deprived of, *light*

This world that has plenty, many fields filled with seed
Wastes the wants of starving children, we fail to feed
Cities filled with skyscrapers stretching from sea to shining sea
Makes no room at the inn for families cast out onto streets
This world with a God who is the Great Healer
Leave their solders with wounds to bleed
Adding to their suffering after they've suffered, so others could
be free
This world where flags wave for freedom
Many remain un-free
Keeping citizens shackled in a lifetime of poverty
Under the name of aid
Adding linkage to their chains
This world has lost its sight
This world has lost good taste
This world in desperate need of change

TWO FOOT. FOUR FOOT.

By Colleen H. Robbins

It started the day I stood on the shore of the Waingunga River, searching the muddy water for signs of crocodiles. A good spot to hunt for wild bullock. I could drive the beast into the mud and kill it as it sank into the mire. The wicked horns would never touch my skin. I dipped my head. It was a good plan.

Baqui ran down the shore toward me, unkempt grey hair falling into his eyes. "Langri, I have news!" He barreled into me. He only came up to my chest, but he forced me to take a half step back to keep my balance.

"Insolent scavenger," I growled. "What right have you to call me by name?" The wind blew across my shoulders, ruffling the striped pelt I wore. I lifted my arm to give him a blow, but he backed away. He started to whine and crawled half behind a bush before regaining what passed for courage among his kind.

"I have news, Great Hunter."

Of *course,* he had news. Creatures like Baqui always had news. They traded what they knew for scraps of food. I knew Baqui stole when he could get away with it. The large notch in his left ear was probably a punishment for thievery.

"The forest tribes, they have taken in a lost child."

"A child?" Now he had my attention. "Is it a changer?"

"I cannot tell. A young couple has taken it in, feeding it with their own offspring."

"The fools. They will bring destruction on us all." I remembered other encounters with the changers. Easy enough to take down from behind, one at a time, they fought viciously as a pack. I killed many of them in the past. There were always more.

I gave Baqui a few scraps to continue. I dealt occasionally with Kela's tribe, very traditional. Perhaps I could talk some sense into them, convince them to turn the child over to me. If it *was* a changer, no one was safe. I wondered how soon the child would develop the sorcerous powers of its brethren. Only one way to tell.

I traveled less than a day to find Kela's territory, even with my injured leg. I stumbled over a pack of changers just before twilight. Their weird yowls filled the darkness. I cut two of them down before they spotted me. The rest scattered just as I jumped the third one. I was lucky. He only got one spell off: my face burned, but not too severely. I holed up to heal for a few nights.

I should have known Baqui would run to Kela. Might as well earn two scraps for the same bit of news. By the time I found the young couple, the scavenger already stood by. I stayed back in the trees for a few minutes, listening to him boast about my hunting prowess. For once Baqui told the truth. My reputation was well-deserved.

The child toddled out of the couple's dwelling for a moment, then dropped to all fours. I could feel the chill travel the entire length of my body. Two foot. Four foot. The child *was* a changer. Couldn't they see the danger? I leapt forward.

"Give me the child." I thought it a perfectly reasonable request.

"I, Raksha, will not let you take him." The mother spoke, her weapons shining as she prepared for battle. The father shooed the child back inside.

I pressed my advantage. I was taller than any in Kela's tribe, and my body rippled with muscle. I backed Raksha into her dwelling and tried to push my way inside. My superior size suddenly became a disadvantage. The small doorway made it impossible for me to enter without crouching and twisting. I could not reach the child without making myself vulnerable. I looked again at Raksha. As fierce as a mother wolf protecting her cubs, her eyes flamed in the dim light. She would attack before I entered halfway. I had lost this round. I backed away. "Kela and the Council will never accept the child among the tribe. Give him to me. He is dangerous. He will hunt you when he is grown."

"It is *you* he will hunt." Raksha's words followed me back into the forest.

Baqui was waiting nearby. I cuffed him away from me. "Tell no one of this or I will hunt you," I assured him. He heard the truth in my words. He scampered away, faster than I could follow with my lame foot, but I was the best tracker in the forest.

I tried to protect them; I really did. I went so far as to search out Kela and insist he call a Council meeting. I had them almost convinced about the danger the child represented. Almost, but not quite.

Raksha refused to stay silent. "What right does a lone hunter have to speak in our Council?" The tribe took up the cry and drowned me out.

"The child is not of our kind. Who speaks for him?" I brightened up. Kela could see the truth. The ancient laws prevented Raksha and her husband from responding to this since they were part of the dispute. The child would be mine within the hour.

"I will." The grizzled old teacher stood where everyone could see him. He was not actually a member of Kela's tribe but held in such reverence that all accepted his word. I hissed in frustration.

"Will no one else speak for the child?" Kela put a hand on the child's shoulder when a soft voice spoke up across the clearing.

"I will buy the child's life. There is a fresh-killed bullock by the stream. Is it enough?"

I looked across the clearing and met Gheera's eyes. A formidable hunter himself, the black-haired one often tried to claim a greater skill than I. I hated him, particularly when Raksha's challenge against a hunter's right to speak was forgotten and they merrily debated his offer.

It took the Council only a few minutes to reach an agreement. They accepted Gheera's gift and adopted the child into the tribe. The tribe would protect him until he was grown. Unless they cast him out.

I walked away. I would return many times over the next few years to watch the child from the underbrush. Two foot. Four foot. Over and over he proved himself a changer, but the tribe became too used to his ways to understand the danger he represented. I spoke with the younger tribe members, pointing out the child's differences. I spoke with the older tribe members and pointed out how differently the child aged. Already he grew into his sorcery. He would be alive long after the entire tribe died unless he was killed. I was the only one who could do it.

When the drought came, the warring tribes called peace. Many of the hunters stopped hunting because the game was just too thin and wary. Gheera and I continued. The changers grew bold. Packs of them invaded the forest at the edge of the fields, driven there by hunger. A few died in the fields, their bodies shriveling in the bright sunlight.

The child crept down to the muddy trickles of water along with the others of his tribe. Everyone could see his differences: skin as hairless as a frog, and an unblinking stare that caught your eyes for hours until you looked away and did his bidding. Slowly the members of Kela's tribe began to listen to me.

A few more years and Kela grew past his prime. His word as leader was the only thing keeping the child in the tribe. When Kela missed a hunt, everything would change. I spoke with the younger tribe members again, directing them to a particularly savage bullock with wickedly sharp horns. The next day Kela found himself facing more than he could handle. It did not take long. The old grey leader took a horn and died of his injuries.

The new leader called the Council that night to complete the change from old to new. I felt a moment of panic when they told me the child had gone hunting alone. I knew what he hunted. He crossed the fields and went into the village. He couldn't help himself.

My panic eased when the child arrived, a small covered pot in his hands. Ten years ago, he came to the forest and now he wore the unmistakable look of a man of the village. I watched quietly as the youngest tribe members started to question his presence. The elders joined in. Everyone could see his difference. Surprised at the hatred and fear I heard in their voices, I realized the child had been using his powers for some time, even among his adopted brothers.

They cast him out that night, cast him out to the wailing of Raksha and her husband. Angry, the child threw down the pot he held. The moss burst into flame, bushes and trees following. I tried to grab him, but the boy thrust a flaming stick at me and beat me over the head. He screamed threats at me. It surprised me and I gave back, my head burning with pain. I had not realized that the boy had come into all his powers. When he ran into the forest and disappeared, I followed.

The trail led back to the village. I waited in the forest. It took less than a week before the men inside the walls drove me off. The boy must have worked his magic on them, too. I left for a month. Sooner or later they would send the boy out to work in the fields.

On my return, I stood aghast. The boy led every cow from the village out into the edges of the forest. How had the changer-- still a youth--convinced the villagers to give him such a gift? His powers were greater than I thought. I needed time to plan. With such a herd I could find him again tomorrow with little effort. Today I would kill an easy meal, perhaps a small pig, and relax while I regained my full strength.

I followed him the next morning as he left half the cattle with a boy from the village and drove those that remained into the edges of the forest. I would have taken one then, but I saw a few of Kela's tribesmen lurking nearby, still under the boy's sway and waiting for his orders.

I knew I could find him again after his bulls wandered away in the forest. I followed the cattle trail back to the village. I found it easy to follow the other half of the herd, and before long I saw them. The cows traveled slowly with their calves, content to chew the grass and scrub that grew near a high-walled ravine. I circled the area twice. If I frightened the cattle into the ravine, they could not escape. I could choose and kill the best and prove to the villagers their mistake to trust any of their cattle to the changer. Herding them into the ravine was easy.

I singled out an older cow and started my stalk. When I closed enough, I would kill her.

My intended victim raised her head. I froze in place. I must have made a noise. She hadn't scented me, for the wind blew into my face. I waited for her to relax. Instead, the others lifted their heads. What was wrong?

The sound of wolves rose from behind a cloud of dust fast approaching me from behind. The ground shook now with the thunder of hooves as the changer boy rode a slate grey buffalo, leading the bulls to rejoin the rest of the herd. Trapped, I looked at the high sides of the ravine, knowing that with my lame foot I could never make the jump. The memory of the boy's voice haunted me from the night Kela's tribe cast him out.

"Run, lame jungle cat. When next I come to the Council, Tiger, I will wear your stripes."

The bulls are closer. My ears are flat against my head. I can do nothing but snarl in defiance. The changer boy Mowgli rides his buffalo. The bulls are not listening to me.

WHAT TIME IS IT

By Tom Hernandez

Time after Time
Time out of mind
No Time like the present
Time flies
Time waits for no one
Wasting Time
Making up Time
Who's got the Time
Time's right
Time's wrong
Time's up
What is Time
anyway
But a tool
To say where
We are
In this second
In this minute
In this day
A way to assign
Value, to
Know what is new and
What to get rid of
As fake as Splenda
And not quite as sweet

Each clock's tick
A new brick
Trapping us behind
Walls of fear, sloth
And arrogance
Each cry for
More Time a

Reflection of
Self-deception
As we vainly refuse
To make Time
For Time
Yet still we honor Time
With the fear and awe
We once saved for our gods
All now lying at the feet of Time itself
Weak, irrelevant or dead
We have faith in Time
In a world where belief is belied
By the reality of fake news
Where Truth seems only to exist with a Capital T
Time is the only thing
Worth the effort
Promising a new day
A new hour
A new minute
A new second
Of grace
Time…
Real as a
Beating heart
a first kiss
a last breath
…is a
Door always open
To the possibility
of *HOPE*
It'll come
Just give
It Time.

BIOGRAPHIES

Denise M. Baran-Unland is the author of the phantasmic BryonySeries. this includes a supernatural/vampire trilogy for young and new adults and its five-volume prequel *Before the Blood*, the Adventures of Cornell Dyer chapter book series for grade school children and the Bertrand the Mouse series for young children.

Baran-Unland has six adult children, three adult stepchildren, fourteen total grandchildren, six godchildren, and four cats.

She is the co-founder of WriteOn Joliet and previously taught features writing for a homeschool coop, with the students' work published in the co-op magazine and The Herald-News in Joliet.

Baran-Unland blogs daily and is currently the features editor at The Herald-News. To read her feature stories, visit theherald-news.com.

To buy her books, read her blog, and follow her on social media, visit bryonyseries.com.

Mauverneen (Maureen) Blevins is a freelance writer and an award-winning photographer. Although she has spent most of her life in the Joliet area, she is definitely possessed of the wanderlust and travels whenever she can, irregularly blogging at MauveOnTheMove.com.

She began writing in high school, but her imagination took her on flights of fancy long before that. She has been published in a variety of publications, including newspapers, anthologies, and magazines and is currently editor and main contributor of The Dashboard, a regional Classic Car magazine.

Her blog, Positively Tuesday, is her small attempt to combat negativity. Her photography work can be seen at fineartamerica.com/profiles/1-mauverneen-blevins.

She has three daughters, and a handsome four-legged companion named Bailey.

Holly Coop resides in Joliet with her family. She is an author and artist. She enjoys writing spiritual and inspirational poetry and motivational quotes.

Coop has self-published three books, *A Cup of Inspiration To Go Please – My Heart Runneth Over*, *Heart Strings – Forever Wander*, and *Locks of Love – A Book of Encouragement.*

She also publishes a blog, writerbeeme.blogspot.com, and has an Etsy shop, hollycoopcards.etsy.com.

Purchase Coop's books at HollyCoopBooks.com.

Diana Estell: The joy and pains of Estell's personal story, as well as her educational background, have shaped her writing style.

Estell has a Bachelor of Arts from Northern Illinois University and it was there, while writing for her classes in anthropology, that her love of writing re-awoke.

Growing up, Estell had a book in her hand constantly. Books like Little House on the Prairie, Little Women, and countless others. The love of words is a deep passion of hers.

She enjoyed reading the dictionary, taking words and changing them into new words. Words were her imaginary playground, a veritable lush garden, springing out blossoms of creativity.

When Star Wars blasted into orbit, so too did Diana's love for all things fantasy. Dungeon and Dragons and Star Trek played a significant role in her private imaginary world. Now the worded playground, with its abundant flora, sprung forth thorns of sharpened steel. Planets and creatures emerged with ease. This passion for fantasy has never left but has grown stronger.

Estell has traveled extensively, most recently to Paris, France. Her love for history, martial arts and weapons is woven into her writings. She has a black belt in a martial arts blend of Taekwondo and Jujitsu.

She had anticipated she would be going on archeological digs after graduating, but childhood dreams never die. No matter how many layers of her past accumulated, nothing could stop a story from emerging in her mind.

Estell's first novel, *Abyss of the Fallen*, is scheduled for release in 2019 by Brimstone Fiction.

Email her at inklings67@aol.com

Annette Gonzales currently lives in Joliet, Illinois, but spent most of her adult life in the Washington, DC area.

She writes very short stories, sudden fiction, poetry, fiction noir, etc., but her favorite writing format is creative non-fiction.

She is the former editor and publisher of *Spiraeas: A Journal of Literature and Art*.

Gonzales holds a Master of Arts degree in Creative Writing and Graphic Design from University of Baltimore and is currently an adjunct Associate Professor at University of Maryland University College's online campus.

Alfredo Gutierrez aka Freddy, is an amateur writer who was born and raised in Texas but currently lives in Monee, Illinois.

He is a lab supervisor at Antech Diagnostics where he helps keep people's pets as healthy as he can.

He has been a member of WriteOn Joliet for three years intermittently.

Gutierrez currently attends PSC and enjoys cosplaying on his free time. He has never been published but hopes to make his dream come true in the near future.

Robert B. Hafey has authored three books. A memoir, Boomhood – A Baby Boomer's Free-Range *Childhood and two technical* books, *Lean Safety – Transforming Your Safety Culture with Lean Management* and *Lean Safety Gemba Walks – A Methodology for Workforce Engagement and Culture Change*.

He also contributed a chapter to the scholarly Routledge Companion to Lean Management and stories for two anthologies written, compiled and published by members of the Write-On-Joliet writer's critique group.

Hafey currently resides in Homer Glen, Illinois.

For more information, visit boomhood.com.

Dale Hansen is retired and spends his time reading, running, mentoring others and watching his grandkids.

He enjoys leading small group Bible studies which he has done for over 30 years. Dale has published two books and is working on his third book about his dealing and living with Parkinson's Disease.

Hansen has enjoyed and learned a lot from the WriteOn group. He is married with two daughters and three grandsons. He lives in Joliet.

For more information, visit:
www.groundedandgrowingweekly.com

Jessica Harris was born in Chicago, has lived across the United States and Europe, and has traveled extensively.

She attended Trinity Christian College & Oxford University and graduated with a degree in history and education.

After beating cancer, Jessica Harris married her amazing husband in a castle (made complete with a groom-led archery shoot).

She currently lives in Florida with her husband and their Newfoundland Dublin. She's written multiple novel-length works and numerous short stories.

Ryan M. Harris was born in Indiana and has lived all over the United States. He and his wife and currently reside in Florida.

His education is in Philosophy, having attended Marion University and IUPUI. Ryan Harris has been writing seriously for about ten years. He writes mostly short fiction in the science fiction and fantasy genres.

Tom Hernandez is a writer, public speaker, performer and communications professional. Born and raised in Joliet, Illinois, Tom has been writing personally and professionally since childhood.

His writing explores the many complicated facets of life — marriage, family, relationships, identity, aging, parenting, faith, social justice and politics.

He and his wife, Kellie have two adult daughters and welcomed their first grandchild in 2018. They live in Plainfield, Illinois.

For more information, visit tomhernandezbooks.com.

Todd Hogan is a writer who grew up in Joliet, Illinois, in a Catholic family of ten kids.

He married his wife, from a family of six kids, at Notre Dame where he graduated. He also graduated law school from the University of Arkansas. He returned to practice law and teach, before working in Chicago in various capacities for a large commercial insurer.

Hogan and his wife have returned to Joliet, living in the same home where she grew up. His published short stories appear in several anthologies.

S. Houk is a poet and award-winning playwright. Favorite themes include celery and gin. She also writes essays, books, and flash fiction. She paints whenever she can, and her recent photography show is entitled "Math & Nature."

When not writing, Sharon can be found doing IT work, teaching at Lewis University, and walking in the forest. She lives in Joliet, Illinois, with her imaginary Irish wolfhounds.

For more information, visit sharonhouk.blogspot.com.

R. Michael Markley lives in the Chicago area with his wife, Kristine, on four acres of land.

He is a former member of the Christian Writer's Guild and a publisher of his own newsletter. Markley's intrigue and knowledge for the Mafia, along with a passion led him to write Necessary Death, story of corruption, deceit, loyalty, and blackmail but with a Christian spin. He is currently working on a sequel

To buy his books, read his blog, and follow him on social media, visit www.rmichaelmarkley.com.

Sue Mydliak lives in Illinois with her husband and has been writing for 10 years.

She started writing when the book "Twilight" first came out and fell in love with the paranormal genre.

Since then, she has written and finished her Rosewood Trilogy and just recently her anniversary edition, "Forever," which is the first book re-written for adults.

She has also published "Southern Shorts," which is an anthology of short stories about Dry Prong, Louisana and "Night Games," another paranormal novel.

For more information and to purchase her books and artwork, visit suemydliak.wordpress.com and fineartamerica.com/profiles/sue-midlock.html.

Kenneth Lee McGee is the pen name of Ken McGee. He was born in a small town in Southern Illinois in 1952. Both parents taught in the local schools. The family moved to the suburbs of Chicago in the early sixties.

McGee enjoyed writing at an early age, but the talent remained dormant and undeveloped for over forty years. He married his high school sweetheart in 1973, worked for a grocery retailer for over thirty years and then retired.

He enjoyed sports as a youth and that continued into adulthood. He played basketball in various leagues until he realized he couldn't compete with the younger players. He found the sport of cycling, joined a local bike club and even joined a racing team. Along the way he and his wife raised a son and daughter.

A few years later, he found his true role. He became a grandfather. Now that he had the time, he resumed writing. He wrote short stories about lost lonely lions, kitty cats who could speak, and puppies who didn't know their own strength for his granddaughter.

Over the years more grandchildren were born. McGee decided to write a story about two kids growing up in the fictional city of South Hampshire. The book turned into the Emmy's Story series and even the spin-off Annie Mercer O'Dell books.

He continues to write under the name Kenneth Lee McGee and credits WriteOn Joliet for teaching him the skills to become a better author.

McGee and his wife of forty-five years live in the Plainfield, Illinois, area, are active in their local church and spend many hours indulging their grandchildren.

For more information, visit kennethleemcgee.com.

James Pressler is career analyst who has lived a double life for the past two decades as a creative writer, exploring the world beyond facts and figures.

His writing comes from a personal passion for storytelling, for offering new perspectives to familiar themes, with moods ranging from friendly humor to serious observations on the darker aspects of life.

Short stories and character sketches have been a compulsion for several years, and several stories have since been published, The first published novel was "The Book of Cain,"with two other manuscripts now being shopped.

For more information, visit writingandtheprocess.com.

Allison Rios was born and raised in Joliet.

Writing has been her relaxation and hobby since childhood, when she began taking notes on neighborhood happenings (the big stuff, like someone mowing a lawn or washing a car) and putting together hand-written newspapers.

She grew into a career in public relations, marketing and web but never lost the love for writing fiction. She has self-published four novels; three fiction and one memoir.

In between a full-time job, chauffeuring kids and shopping for high heels, she spends her free time typing out daydreams and creating new worlds with her imagination – a hobby she likes to share with her children.

Colleen H. Robbins has been writing since she was 9 years old and holds a Bachelor of Arts degree in English Language and Literature from Lewis University.

She has attended numerous workshops, including the Iowa Summer Writer's Conference in 2003, the six-week long Odyssey Fantasy Writer's Workshop in 2007, and TNEO in 2009 and 2013.

Her stories, poems, essays, and articles have appeared under a variety of names in everything from small regional magazines to the gaming-oriented magazines Different Worlds and The Dragon and have been included in numerous anthologies.

She writes both mainstream (literary) fiction and genre (science fiction, fantasy, and horror), and is the author of the Daraga series.

Email Robbins at shavaya@aol.com.

Jennifer Russ is a freelance writer focusing on animal welfare and human rights.

She is the author of "The Heart's Bone," a fictional account of Tibet's youngest self-immolators, and "Whitewallsville: One Man's Journey Through Tigers, Frozen Birds, and Suicide," a story of grief and redemption set within the walls of a mental institution.

When Russ is not tackling the serious topics, she enjoys petting dogs, smelling old books, cosplay, and traveling the world.

Vanessa J.C. Stephens lives in Joliet, Illinois, with her husband and daughter.

She was bitten by the writer's bug in third grade when her teacher gave her a blank hardcover book to fill with words and illustrations for the Young Authors Club. She's been writing in one form or another ever since.

Stephens won the "People's Choice Award" for her play "Down this Time" at the "2nd Annual Emerging Playwrights Festival" in 2019. She was also featured in the Herald News' "LocalLit" newsletter. She has a short story featured in WriteOn Joliet's second anthology published in 2018 and WriteOn Joliet's 2019 Cheetah Anthology.

Stephens enjoys writing short-stories, screen plays, poetry, and is currently working on her debut novel.

Duanne Walton said, "Writing is my gift from God and it's been with me forever. It's seen me through rough times and brought me to WriteOn Joliet where I've found support, encouragement and friends.

"I've also discovered other talents as an intrepid videographer, interpretive dancer (or mime), and comic strip writer/artist. I am blessed and thankful."

www.ingramcontent.com/pod-product-compliance
Lightning Source LLC
Chambersburg PA
CBHW031421250626
47155CB00004B/1579